Astoundingly Audacious Heists 2023

Ray Filby

====================================

Astoundingly Audacious Heists 2023

Publisher : Midhurst

Published by Midhurst

This is a work of fiction.
Any resemblance to actual persons,
living or dead, is purely coincidental.

Midhurst.
2, Freers Mews,
Warwick,
Warwickshire,
CV34 6DP

ISBN 978-1-9168947-5-4

http://midhurstpublishing.uk

Acknowledgements

The author would like to thank his wife , Sue, for proof reading the manuscript and her patience and support during the writing of this book. He would also like to thank the Warwick Writers' Group without whose encouragement and support this book would not have been written. The book has been illustrated by pictures downloaded from the internet from the following sites, Daily Mail, Evening Standard, Getty Images, Glamour UK, London Tickets, Dreamtime, Two Education City, Kent on Line and Geograph Britain & Ireland. The author has written to the sponsors of these websites to clear copyright issues.

Contents

<u>Introduction</u>

The following stories of crimes carried out in 2023 are a series of heists aimed at stealing very high profile artefacts. These items are so important in national life that some of the most senior figures in the establishment had to be involved in retrieving these items. Since the narratives all occur during the year, 2023, there is no point in referring to these establishment figures by just their job titles, Prime Minister, Archbishop of Canterbury, etc, since everyone will be aware of their actual names. Thus, the actual names of these figures are used in the narratives, the Prime Minister, Rishi Sunak, the Archbishop of Canterbury, Justin Welby, etc. However, it must be stressed that this is a work of pure fiction and the words spoken, the attitudes displayed and the actions taken are purely inventions by the author. The author is satisfied that although fictitious, nothing written about any of these characters is in any way detrimental to their integrity as respected figures of national prominence and has written to them to ascertain that they have no objections to their names being used in this way Any other characters appearing in these stories who are not a well-known public figures, are purely fictitious and any resemblance to any other person, living or dead, is purely coincidental.

The Processional Cross

Members of the London gangs, responsible for so much crime in London during the second half of the twentieth century, have now dispersed and can be found in all parts of the United Kingdom. Two of these gangsters, Richard 'Hardman' Harvey and Frank 'Wheels' Morris often meet to reminisce on the things they had been up to during this period which they refer to as the Good Old Days. This doesn't mean that their criminal activity is in the past. Hardman often comes up with ideas for crimes which he considered the pair could safely get away with.

Hardman was heavily built and bald. He was just under six feet tall and had a somewhat aggressive appearance. He was not the sort of person you'd want to take on in a bar room fight. Frank, on the other hand, had quite a contrasting appearance. He was somewhat taller than Hardman. His build was slim and wiry. Frank had a full head of dark, well combed hair and one would assess him as a shrewd individual, ready to take risks but canny enough to recognise which risks were worth taking. At one of these meetings, Hardman reported to Frank that he had responded to an advert which appeared in the New York Times.

"Columbus Museum of Antiquities are ready to pay top prices for historic artefacts to be displayed in the antiquities section being developed by the Museum."

"Where on earth is Columbus?" asked Frank. "The only Columbus I've ever heard of is Christopher Columbus who discovered America."

"Columbus is a fairly large town in the middle of Ohio," explained Hardman. "Its population is just under one million. Columbus is obviously named after the Christopher you mention. Columbus has several museums and the Museum of Antiquities is a new museum seeking to establish itself. I've researched the museum and one of the curators, Joseph 'Kentucky' Guilliamo, is an associate of Angelo 'Scarface' Bellini!"

"Isn't that the Bellini who took over the Mafia when Al Capone was done for tax evasion?"

"No," continued Hardman, "but you're close. Angelo is his grandson. With associates with that sort of ancestry, I considered that Joseph 'Kentucky' Guilliamo is someone we could work with. I've been in touch with Joseph who's responsible for the acquisition of antiquities for the museum. He amazed me as he described some of the items he has on display,

Cleopatra's mummy, the crowns worn by the three kings, the chair used by King Canute when he attempted to reverse the incoming tide, the crown jewels lost by King John in the Wash, the crook used by King David to herd his sheep, Joan of Arc's comb and so on."

"Do the paying public actually believe what they are seeing are really what they claim to be?" queried Frank.

"The general public are very naïve and credulous," replied Hardman. "No-one has queried the authenticity of the three kings whose shrines are in the middle of Cologne Cathedral and the Germans aren't noted for being credulous. To my mind, the claims of Joseph concerning his museum exhibits are no more outlandish than the claim made by Cologne Cathedral!"

"You're obviously telling me this because you think there's something we could do for Joseph and make a bit of money for ourselves on the side," queried Frank.

"I've asked Joseph how much he would pay for the processional cross from Canterbury Cathedral, especially if there were a possibility that this was the cross which St Augustine bore before the procession of monks who landed in Kent to bring the gospel to England." explained Hardman. "He jumped at the suggestion and offered £10,000. I warned him that it would have to be stolen from the cathedral but this didn't deter him. Indeed, he said that if it got a splash in the papers, it would provide the exhibit with an excellent indication of its authenticity."

Canterbury Cathedral

"Isn't Guilliamo concerned that as an admittedly stolen item, the processional cross will be reclaimed?" queried Frank.

"Guilliamo doesn't consider this to be a problem," countered Hardman. "He says that the Museum will return the item, only if the British Museum returns the Elgin Marbles they stole from Greece."

"From all this, I deduce that you're attempting to recruit me as your accomplice in carrying out this theft," answered Frank. "How are you going to set about this heist and how risky would my part in this venture be?"

"You were always a reliable 'wheels' in our London days," said Hardman. "We'll drive to Canterbury in two vehicles. I'll steal a van for this job which I'll abandon near the cathedral. You'll use my car. All you'd need to do would be to park my car near the cathedral and drive off with me when I reach you with the cross. The best car park to use for this enterprise is the Elgar Road car park. It's quiet and only four minutes' walk from the cathedral. If I'm arrested before I get to you, they'll search for my car nearby, exposing you to risk of arrest unless I pretend that the stolen van is the only vehicle involved. Should I not be at the getaway car by 5:00 pm at the latest, you may assume I've been apprehended so just drive off. You'll have had no connection with the attempted crime."

"How will you get hold of the cross?" queried Frank. "Canterbury Cathedral is a very public place and I can't see you using firearms for this sort of theft."

"I shall merely walk into the cathedral in clerical garb, pick up the cross and walk out with it in front of some cathedral procession as if I'm all part of the show! I've done some research.

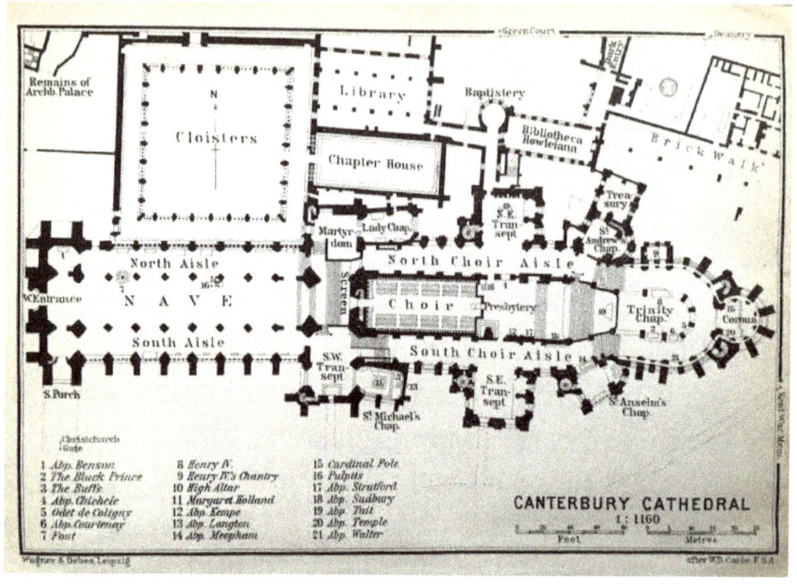

Canterbury Cathedral ground plan

I discover that the Precentor is on holiday during much of August. The choir are doing an exchange with the choir of St. Andrew's Cathedral, Jackson, in the state of Mississippi. They rehearse in the choir stalls on Wednesday afternoons. I'll suggest to their choirmaster that they need further guidance in the way things are done in English cathedrals. I'll tell him that in my role as sub-Precentor, I would like the choir to learn about forming the retirement procession at the end of their rehearsal. There's always a processional cross on a stand at the east end of the choir stalls. When the rehearsal has finished, I'll walk between the choir stalls

Processional Cross

17

holding aloft the processional cross, stop where the choir stalls end and turn around to wait for the choristers to form into a crocodile.

I'll then turn again, lead them down the nave to the north-west door which leads into the cloisters, and then out into these cloisters. When the choir are all are assembled in the cloister walk, I'll say a dismissal prayer whence the choir will disperse. I'll then dump the robes which I'll have borrowed from the clergy vestry and make my way with the cross to where I hope to find you, parked in our getaway car!"

"You seem to have all this very well worked out and I can't see a problem unless you're apprehended as you lead out the choir."

"If I was just carrying the cross, I almost certainly would be stopped but it's most unlikely that any of the cathedral guides, who represent cathedral security, will stop what appears to be an official procession."

"Well," replied Frank, "I'm game for this one. I can't see myself as being much at risk. Either you'll have been stopped within the cathedral or you'll have left the cathedral and made your way to our getaway car. As soon as you're in the car, we'll be off before anyone is aware that something untoward has happened. I've just thought of one problem. You'll be picked up on the cathedral closed circuit TV security cameras and someone will recognise you as an imposter.”

“I've thought of that. I'm going to grow a beard and wear a wig to carry out this heist,” explained Hardman. “I'll be recognised, only as an imposter when the cathedral run through the security tapes later. However, if the police become involved, I'd be recognised as one with form if I appeared without disguise, hence the beard and wig.

Hardman leads procession out of Canterbury Cathedral

So it was, on that Wednesday in August, Hardman carried out the theft in almost exactly the way he'd described to Frank. When he dismissed the choir in the cloisters after they'd completed their processional exit, Hardman didn't just dump his clerical robes. He handed them to one of the senior choir members and asked him to hang them up on peg 15 in the clergy vestry. This was the peg from which he'd lifted them earlier in the day. The processional cross was made in three sections which were screwed into one another. Hardman dismantled the cross and placed the sections into a suitcase which was just the right size and which he'd left by the cloister walk door which opened into the outside world. Hardman made his way to the Edgar Road car park where Frank was waiting in the getaway car. He stowed the case containing the cross into the car boot and joined Frank who was in the driver's seat. As soon as Hardman was aboard, they set off.

On returning to Hardman's house, they congratulated themselves on having pulled off a successful theft without hitch or incident. Little did they know that a police inspector as resourceful as Christine Powers would soon be on their trail.

During choral evensong that evening, it was discovered that the processional cross was not mounted in its usual stand. Canterbury Cathedral is not short of processional crosses and an alternative was soon provided to lead out the choir at the end of evensong.

The following morning, the Dean contacted first the police and then the cathedral insurers. He explained to the police that the cross must have been taken by an imposter who led out the choir after its rehearsal. This imposter claimed to be the sub-precentor. Yes, he was captured on the closed-circuit security cameras but was not recognised as anyone known to the cathedral staff. The processional cross was not excessively valuable. It had cost just under £2,000 ten years ago but was covered by insurance.

Although the Dean played down the theft, this was big news in the local press and was even recorded in the national press and on the local TV news. The Daily Mail provided the most graphic account.

Missing Cross makes Dean very Cross

A daring heist was carried out in Canterbury Cathedral in plain sight of worshippers and tourists. An unknown person, claiming to be the sub-Precentor and officiating while the actual Precentor, Canon Michael Smith, was on holiday, disappeared without trace after processing with the cross. He was leading out the choir of St. Andrew's Cathedral,

Kent constabulary felt that they had no leads to enable them to solve this case and enlisted the help of other police forces throughout the country. Chief Inspector Colin Whittaker, who operated from Oakenhampton in the Thames Valley Constabulary, called in Detective Inspector Christine Powers to see if she had any ideas on the matter.

"The Kent police consider that they've absolutely nothing to go on" said Colin after he had described what had happened. As hoped, Christine came up with a suggestion.

"You say that a stolen van was found abandoned quite near the cathedral," said Christine. "Well, this is a very good starting point. Stolen vehicles are often used to carry out this sort of crime. Do we have a number for the van?"

Colin looked through the brief that had come down to him from the Kent Constabulary.

"Yes. It was a Transit Connect Van, registration KL 57 UPX."

"As police, we have privileged access to the DVLA data base. We can look up the address of the owner," suggested Christine. "I'll get Bill on to it straightaway."

She went out and explained what was required to Detective Sergeant Bill Matthews who soon came up with his report. The van was registered to an address near Chipping Norton and was reported as stolen by its owner on Tuesday! Christine reported to the Chief Inspector the significance for them of Bill's discovery.

"The van is registered to a Cotswold address which means it's on our patch. It's likely that the criminal lives in the area and stole the car the day before the theft of the cross. He would have had an accomplice with him who would have travelled to Canterbury in a separate vehicle and returned with the criminal and the stolen cross back to the Cotswolds."

"Is that going to be of any help in apprehending the culprit?" asked the Chief Inspector.

"This is the sort of situation where the police can be greatly helped by computer technology," explained Christine. "We can use the tapes from the surveillance cameras on the A2, M2, M20, M25 and M40 motorways to run through the number plates of any vehicle leaving Canterbury and travelling in a westerly direction. We can then use the DVLA database to identify which of these any cars are registered to an address with a post-code which lies in the Cotswolds. The owners of these vehicles will give us an initial list of suspects."

The job of identifying the cars registered to a Cotswold address which had left Canterbury and been picked up by surveillance cameras on the motorways as travelling towards the Cotswolds was given to Bill. Just three cars were identified which fitted the search criteria. One of these belonged to a lady solicitor who had travelled to Canterbury in connection with a will for which she was the nominated executor, and another to a couple who regularly visited an elderly parent living in Canterbury. The third one, GP 62 FXY, was registered to a Richard Harvey who was living at an address just outside Chipping Norton. This home had previously been a farmhouse. The name rang a bell in the Chief Inspector Whittaker's mind. He recalled a Richard 'Hardman' Harvey who had form.

The Chief inspector arranged to have transmitted to the station the CCTV footage which showed the cross and crucifer leading the procession which filed out of the cathedral after the choir rehearsal.

Richard 'Hardman' Harvey's car,
GP 62 FXY

"That could be Hardman," he tentatively suggested as he pointed out the crucifer. "If so, he's wearing a wig."

The following morning, Christine and Bill were to be found calling at this farmhouse. Hardman, now clean shaven, reluctantly invited them in when they produced their warrant cards. After introducing themselves by name and rank, Bill started the interrogation as had been arranged between them.

"Can you tell us where you were last Wednesday?"

"I can but that's my business unless you can tell me why you want to know."

"The cathedral processional cross was stolen and a short time later, your car was seen, leaving Canterbury and returning to the Cotswolds. A witness believes that you were seen in the Cathedral," stated Christine.

"Well yes, as a matter of fact, I was sightseeing in Canterbury on Wednesday and as a sightseer, of course I visited the Cathedral. If you think I stole the cross, why wasn't I stopped before I left the cathedral?" Hardman asked. "There were plenty of guides and cathedral staff around who might be expected to stop someone walking out of the cathedral with a processional cross!"

"Well, if you didn't steal the cross, you won't mind us looking round your house will you?" queried Bill.

"I don't mind you looking round the house but on a matter of principle, I won't have the police nosing into my business without a warrant."

Realising that they would get no further with Hardman, they left his house with the threat that they would return with a search warrant.

On returning to Oakenhampton Police Station, Christine reported to Chief Inspector Colin.

"I'm sure Hardman's our man," she said. "He didn't deny he was in Canterbury Cathedral but refused to allow us to search his premises without a warrant. If he has the cross, he'll obviously move it somewhere else soon. I think we need to set up a covert surveillance camera to observe what comes out of his house."

 It took a little while to set up such a camera after dark in a tree overlooking the drive to Hardman's house so that Hardman would have been unaware of its existence but Hardman was ahead of the police. He contacted Frank to appraise him of the situation.

"I can't think how the police knew my car was in Canterbury," he exclaimed. "My car's number must be stored on every surveillance camera in the country since that last time I had a run in with the police. Anyway, we can't leave the cross here. The police have threatened to come back with a search warrant. I'm friends with an elderly and very devout couple, Mark and Jill Scott, who live just down the road. I could quite safely leave the cross with them with a suitable cover story."

Hardman called on the Scotts who were delighted to look after the cross for a few days. They had no idea of its origin and Hardman said that the item deserved a better home while waiting to be collected for a special purpose, than stuffed away in his broom cupboard. Mark and Jill treated the cross with the utmost reverence. It was carefully mounted on the mantlepiece in their living room with the two rods required to convert it into a processional cross standing each side of the mantlepiece. This cross became a focus for their daily devotions.

Mark and Jill Scott

After the cross had been returned to Hardman, Mark and Jill often reminisced about the wonderful special things that had happened to them during the few days this cross was in their house. They had news that their first grandchild had been safely delivered. They received a considerable sum of money from the administrators of Mark's pension fund who had discovered that Mark had been significantly underpaid over a period of several months. Jill was appointed to chair their church's branch of the Mothers' Union and Mark's sister made a remarkable recovery from COPD (Chronic Obstructive Pulmonary Disease).

Things had not gone well for Hardman during the time the stolen cross had been stuffed in his broom cupboard. His hot water system had broken down and he had to have a new boiler installed. A fox got into his henhouse and destroyed his chickens. His roof sprang a leak and required extensive repair. He mislaid the wallet containing all his bank cards and he had the inconvenience of having to wait until these could be replaced. He experienced the serious setback of having the hard drive of his computer wiped clean by a virus. Not being a religious person, Hardman didn't associate these misfortunes with the irreverence he displayed towards the processional cross he had stolen.

The contrasting experiences of Hardman and the Scotts is reminiscent of the Bible story which describes the consequences to two houses which respectively accommodated the Ark of the Covenant on its return to Israel from Philistine territory. While the Ark resided at the house of Abinadab where it was afforded no special reverence, no blessing was experienced. Indeed, when Uzzah, Abinadab's son, disrespectfully grabbed hold of the Ark on its journey from Abinadab's house, he was struck down dead. On the other hand, when the Ark was placed in residence at the home of Obed-Edom, a Philistine, it was treated with reverence and the Bible records that during this time, Obed-Edom and his family were greatly blessed. (2 Samuel ch 6 v 1-11)

Once the cross had been taken to the home of the Scotts to avoid it being observed leaving Hardman's house later on a covert surveillance camera which Frank considered the police were likely to install, Hardman and Fred discussed their future strategy.

"Before we take the cross to the airport in transit to America, we should first use a decoy," suggested Frank. "We can arrange for Mike Smith (*an underworld associate of Hardman and Frank*) to drive your car to Oxford Airport with a package containing a dummy cross to be sent somewhere else in America.

The police will monitor the movement of your car. Meanwhile, we will take the processional cross to Coventry Airport in another car a short while later. If we arrange a delay in getting the dummy cross through customs at Oxford Airport, we'll be able to despatch the professional cross before the police discover they've been chasing the wrong cross."

Frank's plan worked perfectly. When Hardman's car was picked up on the covert surveillance camera leaving his house a few days later, a message was transmitted to an unmarked police patrol car which was waiting nearby to follow Mercedes Benz B Class, registration GP 62 FXY. The car was tracked to Oxford airport where it was lost in the complex parking system.

"No matter," said Chief Inspector Whittaker when this was reported to him. "No need to search out the car. I'll arrange to brief the customs officers and they'll know what to look out for when it's taken through customs, prior to it being dispatched."

Two days later, the box containing the dummy cross was brought into the customs shed. The cross was a cheap altar cross and was addressed to a church in Jackson, Mississippi which Hardman had discovered had recently been burnt down. The cover note in the package described the cross as a present from 'Christian' friends in England. The customs officers thought they had successfully discovered the contraband and contacted Chief Inspector Whittaker who immediately contacted the Dean of Canterbury Cathedral. The Dean sent a member of the cathedral staff to identify the cross and bring it back to Canterbury. Needless to say, everyone was shocked to discover that this was not the expected processional cross.

Two days earlier, the Canterbury Processional Cross was despatched from Coventry Airport to the Columbus Museum of Antiquities. This cross had been collected from the Scott's cottage sometime after the decoy van had started its misleading journey to Oxford Airport. Close attention was no longer being paid to images picked up on the surveillance camera, focused on traffic leaving Hardman's house. This package was described as containing an antique altar cross and passed through customs after the nominal duty had been paid. The customs officers were unaware of the true nature of the cross as the original theft had had little coverage in the West Midlands. They accepted the package for what it claimed to be on the delivery note and were not concerned that the cross was not supplied with a base to enable it to be stood on an altar, its declared purpose. They took no account of the fact that it was accompanied by two rods which could be screwed into the base of the cross to make it suitable for professional use. Thus, the cross was safely despatched to Columbus.

Up until this time, neither the police nor the Canterbury Cathedral staff had any real idea of why the cross had been stolen or its planned destination. As soon as it arrived at the Columbus Museum of Antiquities, the museum authorities launched a great publicity campaign, announcing that an item of incredible value, the cross carried by St Augustine when he landed in England to convert the country to Christianity, had come into the museum's possession. The publicity claimed that although the museum had paid a considerable sum of money to buy this item, it had been suggested that this was an item stolen from Canterbury Cathedral. If this was indeed the case, the museum would not return the cross until the British Museum had returned to Greece, the Elgin marbles it had stolen from there. The publicity paid off. America is seriously short of items of ancient and genuinely historic significance. Crowds flocked to see this item and the museum's outlay to obtain the item was quickly recovered from the paying public.

The Canterbury Cathedral insurers attempted to recover the item but received little cooperation from that side of the Atlantic and came to the conclusion that it was cheaper to pay the Cathedral the £2,000 for which the cross was insured than to embark on expensive litigation against the Museum. The Cathedral was therefore not concerned to pursue the case.

Chief Inspector Colin Whittaker discussed the situation with Christine and Bill. Although they knew beyond a shadow of a doubt that this heist was masterminded by Hardman Harvey, the only evidence they had against him was circumstantial and would not be valid in a court of law to prove their case. Even the video of Hardman bearing the cross out of the Cathedral would not hold up because Hardman had disguised himself and there would therefore be more than a shadow of doubt as to whether or not this person really was Hardman.

"I'm so disappointed for you both," commiserated Colin. "You did an excellent piece of police work in identifying Hardman as the criminal in this case but English law gives so much protection to those being investigated for crime to avoid an innocent person being found guilty, that a cunning criminal like Hardman can so easily evade justice. We'll keep our eyes on Hardman. Make no mistake, at some point, he's going to get careless and we'll nab him!"

When asked to comment of the theft, the Archbishop of Canterbury, the Most Reverend Justin Welby stated,

"It's marvellous how God can defeat the Devil and turn acts of deceit and theft to his advantage. At the end of the day, the processional cross is no more than a thing. What is important is what that thing stands for and how it can impact on others. Knowing what the visitors to the museum will be told about this processional cross, my prayer is that all those who come to view this cross at Columbus Museum of Antiquities will stop to reflect on its significance, that they will hopefully contemplate on how, well over a thousand years ago, missionaries were prepared to follow the cross to the ends of the then known world to a possibly hostile country. May the public visiting the museum come to realise that these monks had made the journey to this country to teach the people here, how the one who suffered and died on the cross, wished to come into their lives to give them new vision and purpose for living!"

The Substitute Crown

Simon Twentyman carefully placed the crown in the window of his upmarket jeweller's shop in the Burlington Arcade. It had cost him nearly £2,000 to have this made but the craftsmen who had prepared this artefact had done a really good job. Simon was confident that in coronation year, this would attract passers by's attention to the window display where most exquisite pieces of jewellery were also on view.

Replica St. Edward's Crown available
from ebay at £1,999.99

The crown was a well-made copy of St. Edward's crown, the Crown of State which the Archbishop of Canterbury places on the King or Queen's head at the climax of the coronation service. The original crown was made for the coronation of King Edward the Confessor who was later canonised to become known as St Edward. It's a very heavy headpiece, weighing 2.2 kg and can only be worn for fairly short periods. This crown was melted down by Oliver Cromwell as a despised symbol of royalty at the end of the Civil War. However, the jewels were retained and the gold was preserved and incorporated into a new crown, commissioned for the coronation of the restored monarch, Charles II. It contains no fewer than 444 precious stones including 12 rubies, 7 amethysts and 6 sapphires. The prime jewel is known as St Edward's Sapphire for it was set the finial cross which surmounted the crown worn by King Edward the Confessor himself. At each coronation where it has been used, various adjustments have had to be made to comfortably fit the head of the new monarch.

This crown seldom leaves the security of the Jewel House in the Tower of London but on the 4th June 2013, it was displayed on the high altar of Westminster Abbey during the service which celebrated the diamond jubilee of Queen Elizabeth II. It was removed again to a secret workshop in Canary Wharf in

December 2022 for remodelling in preparation for King Charles III coronation. While away from the security of the Tower of London, it was closely guarded by specially selected police officers.

The crown was conducted to this workshop in a reinforced van from the fleet of similar vans run by the security firm, SecurTrans.

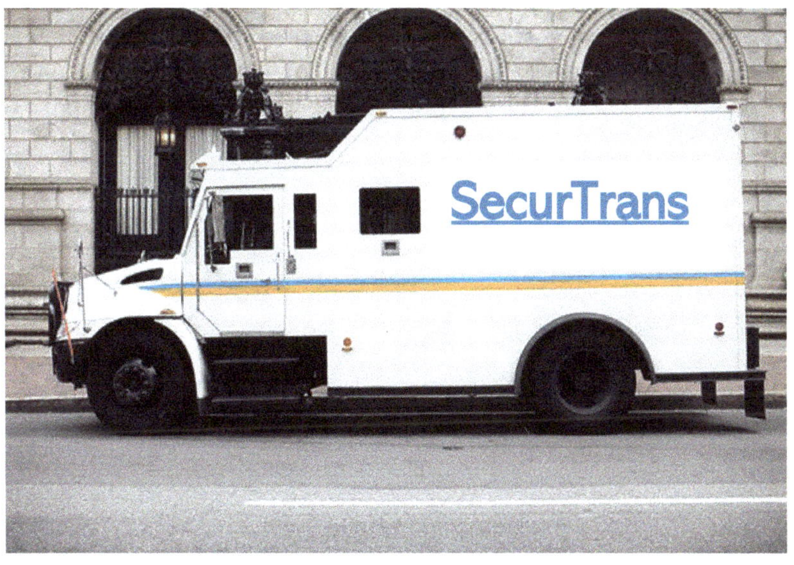

The van was driven by two of the firm's employees, Matthew Roberts and Frank Morris. Frank Morris had been the 'wheels' (getaway driver) of an East London criminal gang and had been arrested during a bank raid which had gone wrong and for which crime, he served two years in Pentonville Jail. Frank Morris was now retired but had joined SecurTrans some years earlier. He had good references from the job he left but, unbeknown to SecurTrans, he had a criminal record which he had concealed from his prospective employers when he applied for the job. When the firm was particularly busy, as it was now, it occasionally called back previous employees on short term contracts to fill any gaps in the service they provided. Frank was now on such a contract and living in temporary accommodation in Bethnal Green which was provided by SecurTrans.

The van drove into the Tower, right up to the Jewel House from which the crown, ceremoniously escorted by Yeoman Warders in their red uniforms, was brought to the van. Matthew and Frank stowed the crown carefully into the van which they then securely locked. Frank paid great attention to the box which contained the crown. In fact, it was rather more than a box but a substantial leather case. It wasn't fitted with a lock. He had a good eye for detail. The van was escorted from the Tower to the workshop in Canary Wharf by two police outriders. This protection was deemed sufficient. A larger escort would have drawn unwelcome attention to the fact that something extra special was being transported. When they reached the workshop, the van was met by the workshop manager. Matthew and Frank unlocked the van and carried the precious box containing the crown into the workshop where two plain clothes officers were already installed.

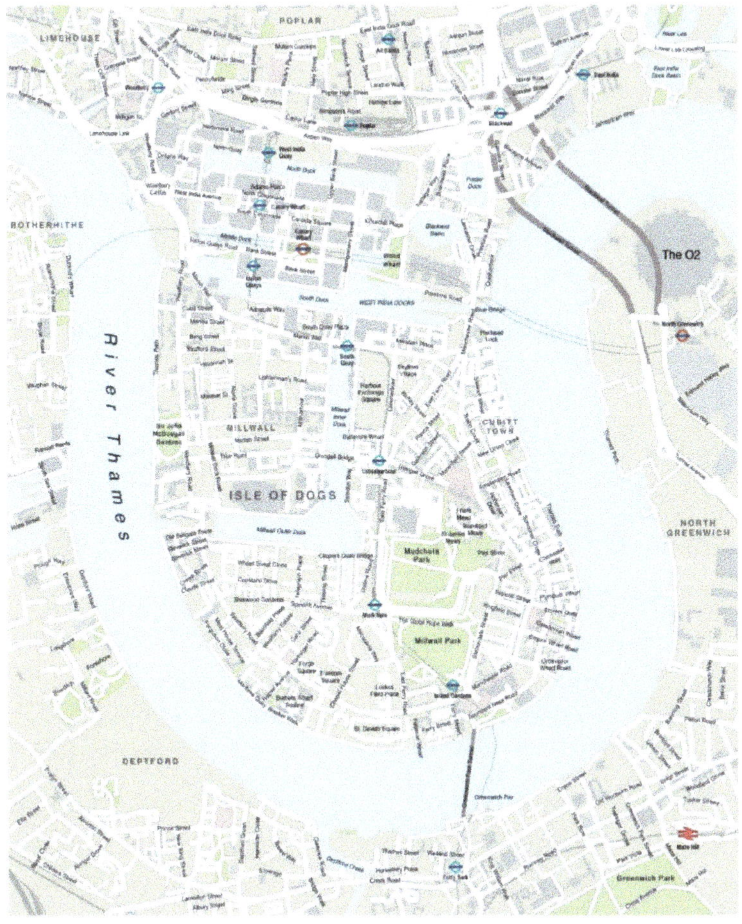

Canary Wharf
41

That evening, Frank contacted Hardman Harvey, his previous boss when he was involved in the criminal underworld. They hatched a plan by which they might be able to steal this crown. It wasn't an item which could be 'fenced' off to underworld colleagues but it could secure a fat ransom.

Dressed in gentleman's attire, Hardman Harvey called at Twentyman's jewellers in the Burlington Arcade and asked Simon Twentyman for how much would he be prepared to sell the crown on display in his window.

"Oh, that's not for sale," replied Simon, "it's just a display item."

"Don't be silly," said Hardman, "Everything's for sale at the right price. You can even buy crowns, similar to the one in the window, from Amazon at £1,650. I'm prepared to pay £2,500 for your crown."

At the end of the day, Simon worked for profit and he saw that here was a chance to make a good profit. They bargained and Simon ended up selling the crown for £3,000. He was surprised to find that his customer paid in cash, carefully counting out £100 notes. In his business, where large sums of money often changed hands, Simon could easily ascertain whether or not these notes were forgeries. These notes were not forged.

Meanwhile, Frank approached a firm of case manufacturers to get a bespoke case made which resembled, as closely as Frank could remember, the case which contained the crown. This cost nearly £700 but when he went to collect it a fortnight later, Frank was pleased with the result. Frank and Hardman now had to wait until the crown was ready to be transported to Westminster Abbey. A week before the coronation, the manager of SecurTrans called in Frank and Matthew to tell them that the time had come for them to transfer the crown to Westminster Abbey. They were to call at the Tower to pick up the remaining royal regalia on their way back from Canary Wharf to the Abbey. The pick-up was scheduled for 10:30 am the following day.

Not many people will be aware of the fact that the interior of SecusTrans vans have concealed compartments where particularly valuable items may be hidden. Thus, in the case of a van robbery, these at least will be concealed from the bandits. Those robbing the van will be in a hurry to make a quick getaway, once they have unloaded from the SecurTrans van everything they can see of value. They won't hang around, searching for something they can't see which probably won't be there anyway. That evening, Frank returned to the SecurTrans yard and loaded the case containing the lookalike crown into one of these concealed, secure compartments in the van which would be used the following day to transport the regalia.

The following day, Frank and Matthew arrived at the Canary Wharf workshop at the scheduled time. Under the watchful eyes of the two policemen present and the manager of the workshop, they lifted the heavy box containing the crown on to the van. The police then went to their motorbikes and the manager returned to his workshop. Frank asked Matthew to go to the police to clarify the route they were to take. Closing the van door behind him, Frank then transferred the case containing the genuine crown into the concealed compartment and placed the case with the counterfeit crown into the main storage area of the van. He then left the van, securely locked its rear door and returned to the cab where he was joined by Matthew who'd obtained the information on the route to be taken from the police. This was hardly necessary because the police escort would be preceding the van the whole way, their blue lights flashing.

When they reached the Tower of London, they drove through the entrance in the Middle Tower up through the Byward Tower and on to the Jewel House.

They Byward Tower

With great ceremony as before, the yeomen warders loaded the remining regalia into the van. This included the sceptre, the orb and the ampulla from which the anointing oil would be dispensed. Once the loading operation was complete, they set off for the Abbey, this time, with a rather larger escort of outriders, motorcycle police following as well as leading this van loaded with priceless treasures.

On arrival at the Abbey, they were met by the Dean of Westminster, the Very Reverend Dr David Hoyle who had been forewarned of their approach.

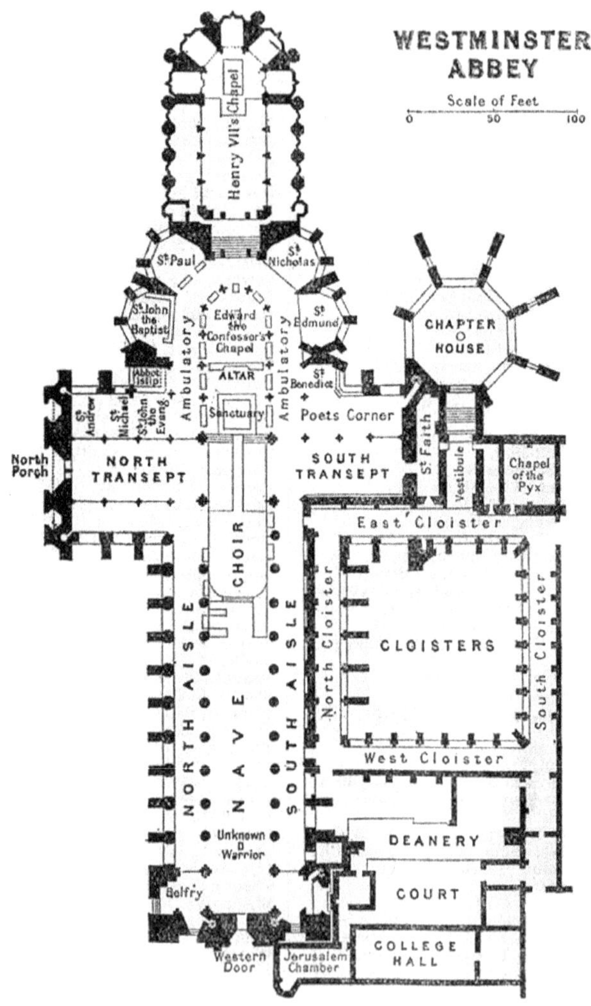

Under the watchful eye of the Dean, the treasures were unloaded by senior clerical staff and transferred to the Pyx Chapel next to the Chapter House. Here they could be securely locked away but still guarded by two police officers located outside the Pyx Chapel and in two-way contact with Scotland Yard. Frank and Matthew returned to the SecurTrans depot. That evening, Frank went back to the SecurTrans depot, collected the crown and took it to the home of Hardman Harvey for safe keeping.

The Dean contacted the Archbishop of Canterbury, the Most Reverend Justin Welby, who was residing at his palace in nearby Lambeth and invited him to come and view the treasures. The Archbishop of Canterbury was the first person to notice anything amiss. He had handled the crown before when he officiated at the service celebrating Queen Elizabeth II's Diamond Jubilee. This was the only recent time that it had been outside the Jewel House in the Tower of London. He froze as he picked up the crown.

"Is this really the crown?" he asked the Dean. "It's nothing like as heavy as the crown which was on display on the high altar at the Diamond Jubilee service."

St Edward's Crown

The Dean couldn't comment, having never previously handled the crown. They called in the Sub Dean, the Reverend David Stanton, but he couldn't voice an opinion. Although appointed in 2013, he didn't take office until well after June when the jubilee service had already taken place. They immediately contacted the guardian of the treasures kept in the Tower of London who came hot haste. He didn't have to pick up the crown to assess its weight. Immediately he saw it, he realised that, beautiful though it was, this was a counterfeit crown. They contacted the Commissioner of the Metropolitan Police, Sir Mark Rowley, and the Prime Minister, Mr Rishi Sunak, to report this dilemma of national importance.

The following day, a delegation of the most senior officials in the land was convened at 10, Downing Street. It consisted of the Prime Minister, the Archbishop of Canterbury, the Commissioner of the Metropolitan Police, the Governor of the Bank of England, Mr Andrew Bailey, the Keeper of the Crown Jewels, Colonel Richard Harold, and the Dean and Sub Dean of Westminster. The meeting was held in the Cabinet Room. Apart from the person or persons who had actually switched the crowns, these were the only people aware of what had taken place and for obvious reasons, this had to be kept secret from the general public. That morning, the Dean of Westminster had received a letter, delivered by courier, stating,

"By now, you will have realised that the real crown has been replaced by a copy, but the real crown will be returned if a ransom of a million pounds is paid. Reply by placing an advert in the Times stating that a specialist was needed to move a valuable item and

leave a contact number. When I ring, I will use the code name, St Edward. "

The Prime Minister introduced those present and explained the problem. The Dean of Westminster read the letter he had received that morning.

"We need to establish precisely when the switch took place," said the Prime Minister.

The Commissioner of the Metropolitan Police had already made enquiries of the police officers escorting the SecurTrans van without disclosing the problem to them and stated,

"Yes, it's important to ascertain just when the transfer had occurred but the only times this could have happened was at the Canary Wharf workshop, the Tower of London and at Westminster Abbey. The police officers had seen that the van was empty before anything was loaded on at Canary Wharf. Nothing was taken out of the van when the remaining royal regalia was loaded into the van at the Tower of London, and the van was completely empty after it had been unloaded at Westminster Abbey."
(The police were unaware of the secret compartments which had been built into the SecurTrans van.)

After some discussion, they realised that there might be no option but to pay the ransom. The Governor of the Bank of England came up with a constructive suggestion.

"We could pay the ransom with specially printed notes. Paper could be used which will turn a very obvious yellow after a few days and the serial numbers could be printed with fluorescent ink which will only be obvious if viewed under fluorescent light. This sum of money in the form of notes will be difficult to launder and as soon as any notes come into circulation, as indeed they must for this crime to be profitable for its perpetuators, it should be possible to trace their source. However, the Bank will have difficulty in producing this quantity of specially prepared notes within the few days remaining before the coronation."

After some discussion, no-one could come up with a better suggestion than that made by the Governor but this would mean that the coronation would have to take place using the fake crown.

The Prime minister addressed the Archbishop of Canterbury.

"Would that make the coronation illegal?"

"Not at all," he replied. "The essential part of the coronation is the symbolism of receiving the crown and the authority it bestows. The actual crown used needs only to appear suitable to be used for as important event as the coronation. Other crowns have been used since Charles II was crowned with the remodelled St. Edward's crown. Indeed, it's only really the most recent monarchs since George V who have been crowned with this particular crown."

After further discussion, the group reluctantly agreed that the only course of action would be to pay the ransom using the special bank notes printed by the Bank of England. As these were designed to be recognisable, it should be possible to trace their source and hopefully recover any money which hadn't already been spent. It was decided that the Metropolitan Police should deal with communication with the perpetuators of this crime. The meeting dispersed with the delegates agreeing to keep each other updated as any significant developments occurred.

Later that day, the Commissioner of the Metropolitan Police rang the contact mobile phone number and said that 'those representing the nation in an official capacity' had agreed to pay the ransom but that it would take a few days to raise a million pounds for this purpose. A date was agreed upon a week after the actual coronation. The ransom was to be dropped off at a specified address in East London and subject to a satisfactory examination of the ransom money, the crown would be delivered within an hour.

Meanwhile, the coronation proceeded without a hitch. It was indeed the wonderful heraldic occasion which everyone expected it to be. The commentators who reported the event on television eulogised over the crown as it came to be used in the ceremony, enthusing at the splendour of the sparkling jewels as the artefact of brass and coloured glass beads was placed on the King's head.

King Charles III wears the
substitute crown

The Bank prepared the package of one million specially minted bank notes according to what had been agreed at the meeting of senior establishment figures. Scotland Yard included a small GPS (Global Positioning System) chip in the package which was delivered at the appointed time to the specified address by two uniformed police officers. Two plain clothes police officers were already set up in an unmarked police car nearly opposite the house, while two more officers had arranged to observe the back of the house from the upstairs window of a property behind the drop off address. One of Hardman Harvey's criminal associates had already been installed in the drop off house with detailed instructions of what he was to do and say should the need arise.

Hardman Harvey had given considerable thought to the drop off arrangements. The house where the drop off was arranged to take place was a Victorian end terraced house in the East End of London. Hardman Harvey owned all the houses in this terrace. A feature of some of the terraced houses in this area was that there was no partitioning wall separating the loft spaces so that one could move from one house to the next and enter or leave the houses via a trapdoor in the ceiling of the landing area. Hardman had been observing the street from an upstairs window of the house at the opposite end of the terrace which incorporated the drop off house. He had seen the unmarked surveillance police car park a few houses down from the drop off house and guessed that the back of the house was being similarly observed.

No sooner had the package been dropped off by a different team of police officers, than Hardman made his way through the loft roof space to the drop off house with the case containing the genuine St Edward's crown. His criminal associate was expecting Hardman to enter the house this way but had no idea what was in either package. Hardman took the package of bank notes and the case containing the crown into another room to examine the contents in private. Without actually counting each note, he ascertained that there were near enough £1,000,000 worth of new bank notes in the package. He also discovered the GPS chip. He repackaged the notes, placed the GPS chip in the case containing the crown and re-joined his colleague in the main room of the house telling him that police officers would call soon to collect the case. On no account was he to open the case but just give it to the police when they called. He told him that it was likely they would ask what had happened to the package they had delivered earlier and where had this case that they were given come from. He was to say that his boss's agent had brought this case round to the back door of the house a short time earlier and had taken the other package with him. He didn't know who his boss was as he only worked through an agent. Hardman then returned to the other end of the terrace via the loft space and phoned Scotland Yard on his mobile to let them know the crown was ready to be collected.

The officers who had delivered the money, received a call from headquarters within the hour, telling them to call back at the house and retrieve another package. When back in their patrol car, they were told to look in the box and report its content. They reported back that something resembling the coronation crown was contained. The police in the car were told to wait while they contacted the other surveillance team watching the back of the house. The police at headquarters were baffled when they reported that no-one had been seen to enter or leave the back of the house.

The officers in the surveillance car were told to safely stow the case containing the crown in the boot and then arrest the man who had carried out the exchanges on suspicion of handling stolen property. They were to have a look round the property to see if the other package was still there or if anyone else was present and then to return to Scotland Yard.

The Commissioner was relieved to have the genuine St Edward's crown safely in the possession of the police, although none of the other police officers were actually aware of the true nature of this crown. He was completely baffled as to how and when the recent exchange of packages had taken place with no other accomplice observed to be involved. The man arrested just stuck to his story that his unknown boss always worked through an agent. He had instructed him to receive the package delivered by the police and exchange it with another package which the agent would bring to his back door soon after the original package had been received. The police had nothing on which they could hold this man and he was duly released after having left his particulars so that he could be re-contacted if necessary.

The story of an audacious and successful crime?

No, the high-power committee of senior members of the establishment who had met earlier had deliberated well. They knew the money had to be laundered and they asked all the banks in the East End to report to them if any large deposit of banknotes was made. Nothing happened for two weeks and then several banks reported that deposits of ten thousand pound's worth of bank notes had been made that morning. They were surprised that such obviously genuine notes appeared to be somewhat yellow. Yes, the serial numbers did show up bright when exposed to ultraviolet light. With the details of how these accounts had been set up, the police were able to find their way to Hardman Harvey's address where he was duly arrested.

Perhaps Hardman had the last laugh after all. Provided the police were prepared to drop charges, he would return the best part of the million pounds ransom money. If they didn't, he would make a laughingstock of senior establishment figures by publicising the fact that King Charles III had been crowned with a fake crown. Hardman never told the police how the exchange of crowns had been carried out so Frank Morris escaped prosecution for his part in the heist.

The Irish Wolfhound

When Frank Morris received a phone call from Hardman Harvey, he guessed that another daring heist was being planned.

"I've a couple of new things at home which I think you'll be interested in," said Harvey.

'This sounds mysterious,' thought Frank as he hurried round to Harvey's home which had formerly been a large farmhouse. As Hardman opened the door, Frank was amazed to see him standing beside a huge dog.

Fergus

"This is Fergus," explained Hardman. "He's an Irish wolfhound. I acquired him from a dog rescue centre. I obtained him for my uncle who loves big dogs and who's recently lost his St. Bernard. He asked me to search out a replacement for him. Although he's big, Fergus isn't dangerous. Far from it. He has a lovely temperament and will make a wonderful companion for Uncle Claude when I give it to him next month."

They moved into the house and Frank became aware of another item he'd not expected. A smart, well pressed army uniform, neatly arranged on a coat-hanger, was suspended from a hook on the door. Two stripes on the sleeve represented the rank of corporal.

"What's this?" enquired Frank.

"This is my nephew, Brendan's, uniform. He's in the Irish guards. He called in here on his way back to his home in Antrim where he's going to spend some leave. He left this uniform, together with other bulky items he didn't want to travel with, here for safe keeping until he returns to duty. In view of what's coming up in the near future, I had a marvellous idea of how Fergus could be put to use with the help of this uniform!"

"And what use might that be?" enquired Frank.

"Well, think of what's coming up on 17th March," challenged Hardman.

"Well, I know that 17th March is St Patrick's day, so I see an Irish connection but I can't see any further than that."

"This St. Patrick's Day will be the occasion when Prince William ceremoniously passes over the honorary Colonelship of the Irish Guards regiment to his wife, the Princess of Wales. This will be marked by a big parade outside Buckingham Palace."

"And how do this uniform and Fergus fit in with that?" asked Frank, still puzzled as to what Hardman was leading up to.

"My plan is that a few days before the parade, we swap Fergus for the Irish wolfhound which is the regiment's mascot and arrange to ransom him back!

"That plan sounds impossible," protested Frank.

"Before rejecting this idea out of hand, let me explain the steps I have taken so far to enable it to be successfully accomplished," said Hardman. "When in London, the Irish guards are usually accommodated in

Hounslow Barracks but with this big parade coming up, they've been moved to the Wellington Barracks by St. James's Park and not far from Buckingham Palace. I've carried out a recce of the Wellington Barracks, dressed in Brandan's uniform. It fits me quite well. As he had left his army identification card in his pocket, I was able to show this to the guard on duty and just walk straight in. I now know where the Irish Guards' mascot is kennelled. He's a lovely animal, officially named Turlough Mor, which is the name of an early Irish king, but around the barracks, the soldiers all know him as Seamus, and this is the name he answers to."

Wellington Barracks

Guards at Buckingham Palace

"My word, that was brave of you!" commented Frank. "I rather imagine you've told me this because you think that I may be able to fill a role in fulfilling your plan."

"Well, yes. You're the best wheels I've ever worked with. We'll use my car as the getaway vehicle and leave it parked fairly near St. James's Park. This is difficult in London but I can book a place at the Adam's House Car Park off Savoy Place on the edge of the Victoria Embankment Gardens. If we leave the Park via the Horse Guards Parade Ground, we can get from St. James's Park to the Adam House Car Park in about seven minutes.

So now to the plan. I have observed the way Seamus's exercise walks are scheduled and it seems pretty random. He's seldom out for more than half an hour and there can be quite long breaks between these outings. He's not always taken out by the same soldier. So, half-an-hour after one of his exercise excursions, I'll enter the Wellington Barracks in this uniform and collect Seamus to take him on a walk. If one does this sort of thing boldly enough with no furtive hint of hesitation, people assume that you are fulfilling a normal duty. I'll walk with Seamus to the far end of St. James's Park where you'll be waiting with Fergus. I'll leave Seamus in your safe keeping and go back to the barracks with Fergus and install him in Seamus's kennel. They'll soon discover that Fergus isn't Seamus. A small bag will be attached to Fergus's collar in which a note will be included, instructing Seamus's handlers to release this dog called Fergus into the Park at 1 o'clock. Fergus will know how to find me. £1,000 must be left in the bag. If the money is found as instructed, Seamus will be released to return to the barracks. Seamus will not be returned unless this money is found to be intact. I'll say in the note that I'm confident that Seamus can find his way back to the Wellington Barracks without help but expect someone to be there to welcome him home.

Lake in St James's Park

Once I've delivered Seamus to you, I want you to take him to the other side of the lake, find an inconspicuous position, out of sight of the barracks but where you can see me. I'll provide meat and titbits to keep him contented until it's time for him to return to his barracks. All going well, Fergus should make his way to me around 1 o'clock. I'll check the money in the bag and if it's OK, I'll signal this to you. You can then release Seamus. This intelligent dog knows his way round the park and will make his way back to the barracks but just give him an encouraging send off, 'Home boy, Home!' Then make your way back to the car as quickly as possible and I will join you with Fergus."

"How do you know that Fergus will find you," asked Frank.

"I've already trained him to answer both to my call and also to an ultra-sonic dog whistle. He's a clever dog. He won't fail us."

So it was, the plan was put into action a few days before the big parade. Corporal O'Brien, Seamus's dog handler, immediately realised that this wasn't Seamus as he approached the kennel to take Seamus on his constitutional and quickly opened the bag on Fergus's collar. He was most alarmed and immediately took the note to the Regimental Sergeant Major who was equally alarmed. They called in the duty officer who in turn involved the Adjutant in deciding on a course of action.

They agreed that they daren't let Colonel Money know what had happened. (Lieutenant Colonel Robert Money was the commanding officer of the Irish Guards battalion stationed at the Barracks.)

"Can this dog be used instead of Seamus?" someone asked.

"Certainly not! Seamus is a highly trained animal and knows just how to behave on parade. A dog like this imposter with no idea of what was expected of him would make a laughingstock of the regiment if he were to appear on parade on this big occasion."

They came to the conclusion that they had no alternative but to pay the ransom but where would they get the money? The guards regiments are well known for the support they give one another when a problem arises, especially if the honour of the regiment is at stake. Whip rounds were held in the officers' and the sergeants' messes and among the other ranks. The money was raised, the greater contribution coming from the officers as might have been hoped.

The first part of the plan worked as predicted. Two guardsmen led out Fergus from the Wellington Barracks to the edge of St. James's Park. On hearing the call and the whistle, Fergus bounded towards the far end of the park where Hardman, still in guard's uniform, was waiting. He petted Fergus as he arrived and quickly checked the contents of the bag on Fergus's collar. Without counting every last note, he could see that there was near enough £ 1,000 in the bag. He gave the prearranged signal to Frank, waiting with Seamus, not too far away but on the other side of the lake. Frank took Seamus to the edge of the lake, let him off his lead and with an encouraging pat, murmured "Home boy, home!"

Seamus paused, sensing his environment. He looked across the lake where his handler, Corporal O'Brien, was standing in front of the barracks, casting his eyes across the park for any sign of his beloved Seamus. Seamus leapt into the water, scattering the ducks with the splash and the tidal wave generated by the large animal leaping into the water and swam across. His handler caught sight of him as Seamus emerged from the water and bounded towards the one whose regular care he enjoyed. Corporal O'Brien was delighted to see his dog back and was unconcerned that he got soaked as Seamus shook the water off himself on to his handler who had knelt to welcome back home the regimental mascot.

The Princess of Wales meets Seamus

Meanwhile, Hardman with Fergus converged with Frank at the Horse Guards Parade as they hurriedly made their way towards the car park. They were suddenly aware that just over two-hundred yards away were four guardsmen in hot pursuit. They reached Adam House Car Park and got into the car in the nick of time. As they sped out of the car park, the four guardsmen breezed up. They were too late to stop the car as it sped off but the sight of a wolfhound, gazing at them from the back seat confirmed that this was their quarry. They attempted to rush after the car but they couldn't catch up with it as it sped away and disappeared into the London traffic which was flowing smoothly around Trafalgar Square. However, one guardsman had the presence of mind to take the car's registration number, GP 62 FXY.

On reaching home, Hardman and Frank congratulated themselves at a job well done and shared the ransom, 50/50. Hardman asked Frank if he would look after Fergus for a few days. In a couple of days' time, Hardman's nephew, Brendan, would be returning to collect his uniform and the other kit he had left with his uncle before continuing his leave in Ireland. If he discovered Fergus, staying at Hardman's house, he would doubtless put two and two together when he returned to the barracks and heard about the heist of their regimental mascot. Knowing that his uncle didn't have an exactly clean record in the matter of law breaking, he would deduce that Hardman was involved in this crime.

Hardman's nephew duly called to collect his kit and returned to barracks. Later, Frank returned Fergus to Hardman which would be given to his uncle, Claude, as a birthday present sometime later in April. With this recent job behind him, Hardman relaxed and started to think ahead about further possibilities of making a quick buck. Unbeknown to Hardman, a police officer, with whom Hardman had had previous encounters, also had a nephew in the Irish Guards.

Detective Sergeant Bill Matthews received a call from his nephew, Lance Corporal Paddy Matthews, asking him if, as a police officer with access to the DVLA database, he could let him have the name and address of the owner of a blue Mercedes, registration number GP 62 FXY. Bill had to inform his nephew that he wasn't prepared to use his position as a police officer to break regulations to obtain details of cars for a third party but in this case, he wouldn't need to access the DVLA database. This registration number was graven on his mind in view of earlier times he had crossed the owner in the line of duty. It belonged to one, Richard Harvey, who lived in a former farmhouse, 'The Homestead' in Barleywheat Lane near Chipping Norton.

On 1st April, there came a knock at Hardman's door. He opened it to be confronted by four burly men who were in fact, Irish Guardsmen in civvies. They were holding bricks. The fact that Fergus had come to the door with Hardman was confirmation to the guardsmen that they'd come to the right house.

"We've come to collect back our £ 1,000," declared their spokesman. "This isn't an April's fool joke. We're serious!"

"I, .. I don't ha .. have your £ 1.000 ," stammered Hardman, no longer the self-confident crime boss.

"We think you have," stated the guardsman. "You'd better find it, quick. It would be a shame for that car to get damaged."

Hardman looked at his shiny Mercedes parked in the drive and then at the bricks the guardsmen were holding. Harvey wasn't in a position to enlist the help of the police.

"I've only got £500 readily available," Hardman bleated. (He'd already shared the other £500 with Frank Morris.)

"Well, you'd better give us the £500 you have readily available," demanded the guardsman, "so that we can count it and you'd better have a hard look for the other £500 which isn't so readily available."

Harvey came out with the £500, still intact from the ransom he'd been paid and then went back into the house. He hunted through his pockets, through drawers, into cupboards. He gathered together all the loose cash he could find which was by and large, the proceeds of earlier heists. £300, £400, £450 he counted out. Some of the cash was in loose coins. He was short of £50 and had exhausted his supply of ready cash.

"He came out with the £450 and assured the guardsmen that this was the last penny in the house. He could write them a cheque. They scoffed at this idea. They took the money and one of the guardsmen hurled his brick through Hardman's front window.

"That's for the missing £50," he said, and the guardsmen went back to their car, parked in the lane, and drove off, never to be seen by Hardman again.

Hardman went in to lament his losses. His Uncle Claude was delighted when he received Fergus as his birthday gift. Hardman never let Frank know that he'd had to return the money. It suited Hardman to have Frank living under the delusion that any heist organised by himself was infallible. We may rest assured that the £950 was fairly shared out as it was restored to the guardsmen who had contributed their cash to save the honour of the regiment.

Princess of Wales
Honorary Colonel of the Irish Guards

The Princess of Wales was made Honorary Colonel in Chief of the Irish Guards in the context of a wonderful parade, set in the forecourt of Buckingham Palace where the regiment, and especially Seamus, did themselves proud.

Kidnapped

A group of decidedly unsavoury looking young men were standing by their motor bikes in the courtyard of a fairly ramshackle building in the middle of nowhere. At one time, this must have been a very attractive farmhouse but now it stood, semi-derelict, by a lane which threaded through fields extending to distant townscapes which could be observed on the horizon. This group of young men looked like typical bikers but they were a muster of anarchic discontents who hadn't found a worthwhile purpose for living. They described themselves as Putin's Proud Protagonists (3P's), a name designed to eschew popularity.

Putin's Proud Protagonists

They had given themselves dinosaur nicknames which alliterated with their first names. The leader of the group was 'Tyrannosaurus' Tony, usually abbreviated to 'Tyro'. A tall group member was 'Diplodocus' Dave, generally referred to 'Dippo'. Others included 'Stegosaurus' Steve (Steggo), 'Brontosaurus' Bill (Bronto) and 'Pterodactyl' Pete (Dacto).

The group had developed a technique for robbing small businesses which, up until now, had proved to be both lucrative and effective. Anything between nine and a dozen of them would suddenly converge from different directions on their motorbikes. They would congregate round the shop or business which was their target for robbery, two or three would dash into the shop, push the shop-keeper out of the way, grab the till takings and return to their bikes, at which point, the whole gang would speed off, the members endeavouring to take as many different directions away from the site as possible. In this way, no obvious single direction in which the group had exited could be identified by passers-by who might be called upon to describe what they had witnessed. The bikes were all fitted with false number plates so that even if a passer-by had had the presence of mind to note down the numbers which should have identified the bikes' owners, it would have been to no avail. To give themselves respectability, the group claimed that they only robbed businesses which were making extortionate profits and gave much of the proceeds of these robberies to the poor. In reality, they robbed any business which looked like being a soft target and the amount given to the poor to earn a vestige of respectability was paltry. They certainly couldn't be compared to the group of outlaws which gathered round Robin Hood.

The discussion which took place as this group gathered after a recent robbery was fairly acrimonious.

"How much did we pick up today from that newsagents?" asked Tyro.

"£237 in notes and a bit of small change," said Dippo who managed the cash for the gang. "I don't think that Andover was a particularly affluent area to target. The trouble is that so many people pay their way these days using bank cards, that very little loose cash ends up in the tills."

"Well, £237's a bit better than the measly £96 we picked up at the barber shop in Swindon," commented Steggo, the one who could usually be expected to give an optimistic appraisal on the results of the group's activities.

"We're not doing nearly well enough," stated Tyro. "Small pickings like that will barely keep us in booze and smokes and enable us to keep petrol in our tanks. We've got to have a major rethink. We need to identify a target which'll be really profitable."

The group stood around for a time in glum silence. Then Bronto spoke up.

"As you know, I've a secret contact in London who really knows what's going on from the inside. We haven't made much use of the info he's passed on recently but the latest news he's discovered is that the royal children are returning to their parents, the Wales's, in Windsor after the weekend. They'll have been spending time with their Uncle Edward and Aunty Sophie (*Duke and Duchess of Edinburgh*). They'll be travelling sometime during the morning of Monday, 7th August. There are only two roads they could use, the A4 or the M4. I reckon we could kidnap Prince George and ransom him for thousands of pounds. It'll be a tough assignment. They'll obviously have an escort but I'm sure we could manage it."

"Now you're talking," said Tyro. "Sounds a good idea to me."

Dacto dissented.

"I don't mind taking the proceeds of rich businesses which are robbing their clientele with unreasonable charges but I draw the line at putting kids' lives in danger."

Tyro asserted his position as accepted leader of the group to override Dacto's objection.

"Prince George's not a kid. He's a spoilt royal brat. I vote we go along with Bronto's suggestion, but we can't pull this off without careful planning."

Tyro's 'vote' was an authoritive edict to the group which allowed no further dissent.

A few days later, Sir Mark Rowley, the Metropolitan Police Commissioner, received a letter marked top secret and URGENT. It had been sent by Dacto who signed it with 3P's designed into a simple monogram. The note read:-

If I tell you that I know that the children of the Prince and Princess of Wales are scheduled to drive from London to Windsor on the morning of Monday, 7th August, you will realise that this note is written by someone who has access to privileged information and is therefore genuine.

A gang is planning to kidnap Prince George and demand a ransom for his safe release. Please don't solve this problem by changing the travel arrangements for if this is done, the gang will realise that as their only dissenting member, I have contacted the authorities. I will then be in danger of being killed or even worse may befall me. Rather, make sure that the car used to transport the royal children is adequately guarded.

Sir Mark immediately contacted the Personal Protection Officer (PPO) at Buckingham Palace who we can know only by his code name (Bert Prothero) and a meeting was convened to discuss strategy. In the interest of security, Bert, the PPO, was in favour of rescheduling the journey to a different time but Sir Mark pointed out the danger in which such an action would put his source. Also, with the formidable team they would have in place, they stood an excellent chance of apprehending a disruptive criminal gang which had evaded capture for far too long. They agreed that a convoy, consisting of three cars and two motor cyclist outriders, should have several armed officers in the cars preceding and following the armoured limousine in which Prince George, Princess Charlotte and Prince Louis would be travelling, but in reality, the children in the car would be royal lookalikes. Also travelling with the children would be someone appearing to be the royal nanny but who in fact was an experienced woman police officer. She would be briefed that whatever happened during the attempted abduction, she was on no account to leave the side of the one posing as Prince George.

"I don't think you'll have any great trouble in recruiting a woman police officer to take on the role of royal nanny, but how will we recruit the children?" asked Bert. "I can't imagine many parents being prepared to put their children to that risk."

"I'll make discreet inquiries in that direction," replied Sir Mark. "I'm aware of several police families whose royalist sympathies are so strong and who have implicit faith that the police can pull this one off safely, that I think I can find three ideal children. I already have in mind a woman police officer who would admirably fill the role required."

"So it was, three suitable children, who we will refer to from now on by their alias names, 'George', 'Charlotte' and 'Louis', were recruited. (Their real identities can never be disclosed.) The nanny was Detective Inspector Christine Powers, a policewoman well known beyond the Thames Valley Constabulary.

She would take on the alias name of 'Nanny Macpherson'.

Prince George, Princess Charlotte and Prince Louis

How were Christine and the children going to be prepared for the dangerous task which lay ahead?

As it was school holiday time, there was no need to arrange for them to take time off school. A plan was set up by which the four of them would live together in a safe house for a week where they would bond. During this time, they would not use their real names but get used to being known by the names they would assume for the task which lay ahead.

The time spent in the safe house worked out well. The children had been well selected. Not only did each have a more than tolerable resemblance to the prince or princess they were to impersonate, they were intelligent, well behaved and cooperative. The foursome spent a lovely week, playing games, going on outings and visiting Macdonald's, so that by the end of the week, they had wonderfully bonded and quite naturally responded to their assumed names.

Monday, 7th August arrived. The three children and 'Nanny Macpherson' had arrived at Buckingham Palace the previous night and they all slept surprisingly well in view of what they knew awaited them the following day. Looking very much like a family of royal children and their nanny, they entered the royal limousine at 9 o'clock. A secret microphone, speaker and miniature radio transmitter had been sown into 'Nanny Macpherson's' jacket together with a GPS (Global Positioning System) chip. Attended by their escort cars and motor cyclist outriders, they set off for Windsor. A helicopter hovered above the cars and tracked the convoy as it set off.

A member of the 3P's gang, Steggo, had been posted on Hammersmith Bridge to check on the route that the royal convoy would follow.

Royal convoy leaves Buckingham Palace
On way to Windsor

He contacted Tyro using the intercom built into his motor-cycle helmet, stating that the royal convoy was following the M4 motorway. This enabled Tyro to deploy his gang. They made their way to M4 junction 5 and waited for the convoy to pass. They set off in pursuit, the gang's van overtaking the convoy and slowing down in front of the motorcycle outriders. Other members of the gang on their motorcycles rode in thick formation by the side of the royal convoy, preventing it from pulling out and overtaking the van which was drawing to a halt in the left-hand lane. The police were aware that a holdup was planned to take place on the route and they were briefed that although they were armed, in the interests of the safety of the children, they should not fire their weapons unless it was obvious that no alternative was possible to safeguard the children's safety. Should the police escort be unable to thwart the 3P's gang at the point of hold up while at the same time, safeguarding the children, the best chance of safely apprehending the gang would be for a specially selected group of elite SAS (Special Air Service) soldiers to storm the gang's hideout at night when most of the gang would be asleep and their guard would probably be down.

The rear doors of the van sprang open. Two members of the 3P's gang brandishing sub-machine guns jumped out. The police in the convoy cars, also brandishing weapons, simultaneously leapt out of their vehicles. The police were alarmed to see something they hadn't anticipated. The gang members were all wearing explosive suicide vests.

Tyro, one of the gang who had leapt out of the van, started to give orders.

"Prince George is to alight from the car. Should any of you pigs (*police officers*) choose to fire your weapons, we'll set off our suicide vests and all of us will be blown to hell."

Princess 'Charlotte' started to cry. Prince 'George' and 'Nanny Macpherson, alighted from the limousine, 'Nanny Macpherson' holding on firmly to Prince 'George's' hand.

'Nanny Macpherson' surveyed the gang. She knew enough about weaponry to realise that most of the gang were carrying imitation guns but the sub-machine guns, carried by the two who had jumped out of the van, looked like the real thing.

"You, Nanny," commanded Tyro, "get back in the car!"

"I'm not leaving my Prince," declared 'Nanny Macpherson', "and if you attempt to separate us, I'll set off the suicide vest of anyone who comes near us."

'Nanny Macpherson' was 95% sure that, like so many of the guns arraigned against them, the suicide vests were dummy.

Tyro was 100% aware that the suicide vests were dummy and a game of double bluff was being played out. If the 'Nanny' attempted to set off a suicide vest on one of his gang and nothing happened, it would be immediately obvious that the vests were dummy. He surveyed the firepower of the opposing sides. The police with real weapons would easily outshoot his gang members, most of whom were armed with no more than dummy guns.

"All right then, Nanny, get in the van with Prince George," ordered Tyro.

'Nanny Macpherson' and Prince 'George' climbed into the back of the van. Tyro got in with them and the van sped off. A gang member with a real gun fired into the front tyres of the motorcycles and the three cars. The gang members sped off on their bikes.

The helicopter followed the van. The van left the motorway at the next exit and made its way to a prearranged wooded area. Tyro was aware that a car bearing royal children would be supported by a helicopter but he would fool the helicopter pilot. Under the cover of the trees, Tyro got out and ordered 'Nanny Macpherson' and Prince 'George' to get into the back of another van. Tyro got into the driver's seat and waited while the original van set off. A brightly coloured insignia had been painted on the van roof and Tyro fully expected the helicopter to follow this van. After a few minutes, Tyro set off in the other van. As the driver, he was not aware that the helicopter was following them at a distance. The helicopter pilot had been briefed to follow the signal from the GPS chip rather than the van. Tyro was disconcerted to see a helicopter hovering nearby when he reached the derelict farmhouse which was their headquarters. The gang on the motorcycles had arrived back, ahead of Tyro.

Putin's Proud Protagonists' Headquarters

'Nanny Macpherson' and Prince 'George' were let out of the van and shown to an upstairs room in the farmhouse. It was sparsely furnished with just a chair, a table and one bed. In view of the age and dilapidated state of the building, this room surprisingly did have an en-suite washroom and toilet. The door was locked behind them. 'Nanny Macpherson' surveyed the room to see if any bugging device had been installed but none was apparent. The room was so sparsely furnished that it would have been difficult to conceal such a device, but in any case, the gang had not seen any necessity to listen in to Prince George whom they had expected to be in isolation in the room..

Prince 'George', who had been very brave up until this time, now looked extremely worried but 'Nany Macpherson' was able to placate his fears. In a low voice, she explained to him that the police knew exactly where they were because she had a GPS chip sewn into her clothes and that she also had a concealed radio which she could use to communicate with the police without the gang members being aware that this was possible. She told him that the rescue would come about in the middle of the night when the gang were all asleep.

'Nanny Macpherson' then used her concealed radio system to quietly confer with Sir Mark Rowley who was coordinating this sensitive exercise. She was relieved to hear that the police were aware of the derelict farmhouse where she and Prince 'George' were being held. She explained to Sir Mark that from the observations she had made on being taken into the house and the view from the window, she believed that she was being held in a first-floor room to the immediate right of the front door. Sir Mark told her that an SAS unit would be effecting a rescue at 3:00 a.m. He advised her to barricade the door using the bed and anything else in the room which was heavy. The gang were likely to bring out Prince 'George' as a hostage, once the rescue had started.

"Once the rescue has started," he advised, "and there will be no doubt that it has started because it will be a very noisy affair, get yourself and Prince 'George' as far away from the door as possible. If they can't get in, a gang member may start to shoot through the door in desperation."

'Nanny Macpherson' and Prince 'George' continued to speak quietly together. She explained that Sir Mark, the Metropolitan Police Commissioner, had recommended that they should use the bed to barricade the door before they turned in. She told Prince 'George' that he should sleep fully clothed in the bed while she would try to snatch some sleep in the chair but explained that she would wake up Prince 'George' just before 3:00 a.m. when the rescue would take place. They should huddle in a far corner of the room until the police let them know it was safe to come out.

Half-an-hour later, they heard the door unlock, a knock on the door and one of the gang came in with a tray bearing jam sandwiches, a jug of milk, a pot of tea and two cups. Without saying anything, he put the tray on the table, looked around the room and went out, locking the door behind him. 'Nanny Macpherson' and Prince 'George' made the best they could of this frugal meal and spent the next part of the evening in quiet discussion and playing cards. 'Nanny Macpherson' had had the foresight to bring along a couple of packs of standard playing cards and there seems no limit to the games that can be played with these.

At 8:00 o'clock, 'Nanny Macpherson' suggested that it would be a good time for 'Prince George' to turn in but they first used the bed and chair to firmly barricade the door as advised.

"I'll have to wake you in the middle of the night so that we may quickly escape with those who are coming to rescue us. That's why you have to go to bed with all your clothes on and we're keeping the light on," she explained in a whisper to 'Prince George', "but we must first say a prayer that God will ensure that this evening will end well and that we'll be free and unharmed tomorrow."

Prince 'George' readily agreed. He came from a home where prayers were regularly said, both in the morning and the evening. So, after a few moments of quiet in which 'Nanny Macpherson' recollected that whatever the situation in which they now found themselves, they were in the hands of a loving God whom they trusted to bring the outcome of their present situation to a good conclusion in line with his purpose, 'Nanny Macpherson' prayed aloud but in a quiet voice.

"Heavenly Father, we entrust ourselves to your love. We thank you that You have the power to protect us and we look forward to the time, later this evening, when our friends will rescue us from being held in this house. We pray that Charlotte and Louis and the mothers and fathers of all of us may not feel anxious but have the same confidence that we have in Your power to rescue us. We pray for those evil men who have brought us to this place, and pray that as they are brought to justice, they may see how wrong they have been. May this lead them to search out Your better way for them to spend their lives. We pray this in the name of Jesus who died for us to enable us to live wonderful and fulfilled lives, Amen."

As 'Nanny Macpherson' prayed, whatever anxiety 'Prince George' may have felt subsided, and he soon slumbered off into a peaceful sleep. It had been a tiring and tense day for him. 'Nanny Macpherson' couldn't sleep. She knew that a long anxious wait lay ahead and she kept herself awake by playing patience with the pack of cards she'd had the foresight to bring with her. She frequently looked at her watch as the seconds, minutes, hours ticked by. At quarter to three, she woke 'Prince George' and they sat at the far side of the room, away from the door, excitedly waiting for signs that their rescuers were at hand.

The rescue that had been planned was to follow the pattern which had been used to end the Iranian embassy siege which had taken place in 1980.

The 3P's gang had become inured to the sound of the helicopter, hovering nearby. They didn't like it but what could this do while they held Prince George. Three SAS men were lowered from the helicopter to land quietly and safely on the farmhouse roof. They attached ropes to secure, fixed points to enable them to abseil down. At 3:00 a.m. precisely, the rescue started. The farmhouse was suddenly bathed in light from a set of floodlights which must have been quietly installed earlier in the night. The three abseiling SAS men swung out from the farmhouse, returning feet first to smash into windows on the first floor but avoiding the one where the light was still on and which was where 'Nanny Macpherson' and Prince 'George' were believed to be being held. At the same time, two more SAS officers with a battering instrument broke into the front door. All this created a tremendous racket. 'Nanny Macpherson' and Prince 'George' heard their room being unlocked but whoever was outside found that they couldn't open the barricaded door.

SAS men storm 3P's headquarters

"Let me in!" yelled a voice from outside but 'Nanny Macpherson' and 'Prince George' remained tensely rooted in the corner of the room.

Three shots were fired through the door, the bullets ending up harmlessly embedded in the opposite wall. Another shot was heard, accompanied by a yell from outside the door. Outside the house, the police and SAS men were bundling members of the 3P's gang into police vans which had suddenly drawn up outside the farmhouse. One person was carried out on a stretcher. This was none other than Tyro, the gang leader, who was the one who fired through the door and who, in turn, had been shot in the leg by an SAS man. The SAS had been briefed only to shoot to kill if their own or other life was in danger from a gang member. This was an important safeguard to avoid the loss of innocent life when a victim could so easily be confused with a legitimate target in the mayhem and confusion which followed the storming of a hideout by the SAS.

Then, for a short while, all seemed eerily silent. After quite a few seconds had elapsed, a voice from a loud hailer could be heard outside.

"Nanny Macpherson' and Prince 'George', this is Sir Mark Rowley speaking. It's now safe for you to come out."

Sir Mark realised that it was important for the time being to use the alias names of the two who had been abducted.

'Nanny Macpherson' and Prince 'George' removed the barricade from the door and made their way out to be greeted by Sir Mark and other senior police officers. They were shown their way to a large and comfortable police car and driven to the headquarters of Thames Valley Police. Here, Prince 'George' was reunited with his real mother and father, and 'Nanny Macpherson' was greeted by her own anxious parents together with her boss, Chief Inspector Whittaker, and her partner, Detective Sergeant Bill Matthews. Princess 'Charlotte' and Prince 'Louis' had already been reunited with their parents. On her return home, Detective Inspector Christine Powers made herself a hot cup of coffee and went straight to bed to enjoy a relaxed, twelve-hour, deep sleep before reporting back for duty at Oakenhampton Police Station, later the following day.

This attempted kidnapping involving royal personages is a matter that Buckingham Palace and the police would rather keep as much out of the public eye as possible but it was obvious that a big incident had taken place on the M4 involving a royal limousine and the press were demanding to be given details they could publish. A careful press release had to be prepared.

Attempted kidnap of a member of the royal household.

On Wednesday morning, an attempt was made by the notorious 3P's gang to abduct a member of the royal household. The gang was armed with automatic weapons and wore explosive suicide vests. This attempted abduction failed

When asked to comment on the action, the spokesman for the team of SAS soldiers who had carried out the rescue said that they were particularly proud to have carried out this action because thy felt that this was something they could do to honour two very special SAS soldiers who had died earlier in the year. Alec Borrie died on 21st May, aged ninety-eight. He was a founder member of the SAS and had spent much of the 2nd World War behind German lines, aiding the French Resistance in carrying out acts of sabotage. Mel Parry was a member of the team which stormed the Iranian embassy in 1980. He died the day after Alec on 22nd May.

Is this the end of the story? Not quite. The parents of all three children involved as decoys in this incident were remembered in the honours list. The citation extolled their exceptional service and devotion to members of the royal family. Detective Inspector Christine Powers was awarded the OBE (Order of the British Empire) and her citation mentioned the courage she had displayed in performing an act of service to the royal family which was well beyond her normal call of duty.

The members of the 3P's gang were tried for treason which is the description of an act to abduct one, who in normal circumstances, may be expected to become King of England. In a previous age, this would have been a capital crime meriting the death sentence. They were all given life sentences and confined in different prisons. Dacto was included in the sentence to preserve his anonymity as an informant. He had crimes to answer for, committed by the gang before the attempted kidnapping of Prince George. However, he was released after just one year's imprisonment.

The FA Cup

Richard Hardman Harvey and Frank Morris met up, ostensibly to reminisce on what they nostalgically called 'the Good Old Days' when they were both involved in the East London crime scene. On these occasions, Hardman invariably came up with a suggestion of a heist to be pulled off which Frank initially felt was impossible. The suggestion Hardman made this evening evoked just such a reaction.

"I think we could demand a tidy ransom if we could 'misappropriate' the FA Cup!"

Hardman avoided referring to actions he suggested as 'stealing' and used euphemisms like 'misappropriate'.

"I don't think that's possible," was Frank's predictable response. "It's almost certainly in Liverpool's trophy room at present but that room isn't accessible to the general public. It may well have been moved from there to the FA headquarters in preparation for this year's Cup Final which is now fairly imminent. Without a lot more inside information, I can't see how we could possibly start to plan to get hold of it."

"We don't need that information. We all know where the Cup will be on June 3rd and I don't think it will be too difficult to take it then," Hardman confidently asserted. "The difficulty with any endeavour involving the payment of a ransom, is in arranging a safe means of collecting the ransom.”

“Go on, then! How do you propose getting hold of the Cup in full view of thousands of fans at the ground, let alone those viewing the event on television?”

Hardman was eager to explain his plan for stealing the FA Cup.

The FA Cup

“After the Cup has been awarded, there invariably follows a fairly chaotic time after the winning team has been photographed, when the players run round the pitch, brandishing the Cup before the fans. Every player in the team gets their hand on the Cup during this impromptu ceremony. I've been in touch with some of our East London colleagues who have sent me pictures of their sons and other young men who resemble players in this year's final. I think we could recruit their services to enable us to get our hands on the Cup. I've managed to get hold of a dozen Cup Final tickets at some expense but this will be more than covered by the ransom we expect to collect. We are helped by the fact that supporters attend matches wearing their club's team shirts. I have already had a look through the pictures of the young men who can help us in this enterprise and I've come up with ten reasonably close lookalikes to ten of the players in the two Cup Final teams. I'll get hold of five Manchester United and five Manchester City shirts bearing the names of players who will be involved in the Cup Final. Even if not as players competing in the match, they'll be there as substitutes who resemble the young men I hope to recruit."

Frank was now all attention.

"This sounds promising but just how will you get your hands on the Cup and escape out of the ground?"

"The young men I will recruit will arrive at Wembley looking just like any other supporter, coming dressed to support their team on the day. However, under their tracksuit bottoms, they will be clad in football shorts and socks and be wearing trainers which could pass off as possible football shoes. I'll even get the clothes slightly muddy so that they'll look as if they've been through a match.

Wembley Stadium

Once the real players have had about ten minutes, rushing round the pitch, showing off the trophy to their fans, this activity will get a bit more subdued. Television cameras then usually switch to 'on the pitch' interviews. At a point which I consider appropriate, I will signal to my team. The five who are wearing the strip of the winning team will move to the stand where the opposing supporters will have been. wearing the strip of the losing side. They will remove their track suit bottoms as unobtrusively as possible and hand them to the other five members of the team. They will then get over the barrier and run on to the pitch. Then, I will also run on to the field, dressed in a track suit and carrying a sports bag which will make me look just like a trainer, coming on to the field to deal with an injury. The sports bag will contain a fake FA Cup lookalike.

An FA Cup Replica
Available from ebay at £895

The members of my team will endeavour to get their hands on the Cup to join in the celebrations, keeping well away from any player whose name is the same as the one on the back of their particular shirt. Fortunately, the names are emblazoned on the back and not the front of football shirts. Once they have their hands on the Cup, and this will involve having the lid as well, the five of them will gather round me in a huddle so that, unseen by the crowd, I can change the real FA Cup with the fake one which will be in my sports bag. They will then break from the huddle and carry on prancing around with the fake cup until they can hand it on to a genuine member of the team. I will then exit from the ground, preferably via the players tunnel, and the five members of my team on the field will return to the other five to retrieve their tracksuit bottoms and join the crowd leaving the ground.”

“What are you going to pay the ten lads you are recruiting for this escapade?” asked Frank.

“I think they’ll be more than happy with £1,000 each and tickets to the Cup Final,” replied Hardman. “We’ll be able to demand a ransom of tens of thousands of pounds from a rich football club who will be anxious to avoid the shame of being the team that allowed the FA Cup to be stolen from under their noses.”

"I can foresee a problem," countered Frank. "The key to the success of this venture is your being able to invade the pitch with your sports bag to join your five bogus footballers. Getting on to the pitch at that stage of proceedings won't be a problem but Wembley security staff will never let you into the ground carrying a heavy sports bag. At the very least, they'll want to see what's in the bag."

"I've thought through that one," replied Hardman. "Security at Wembley may be tight on match days but during the week, vans come and go, bringing the food and drink, necessary to supply the catering outlets, without any checks being made. Most of the catering outlets are located on level 2 of the stadium. On an occasion when I know that two or three different suppliers will be making their deliveries, I will infiltrate the delivery men carrying my bag as if I was part of the delivery team. With more than one van delivering, each crew will consider that I am delivering for another firm. I have discovered that there are a large array of lockers behind the catering outlets for workers to stow their clothes and belongings. These are available for casual workers who are only there for the day. The key in each door of these lockers can only be removed, once the door is closed and locked. I have already locked and taken the key for locker No. 201. Sometime before the Cup Final, I'll enter the stadium during a catering delivery slot and lock the bag containing the dummy FA cup in this locker. I'll retrieve it on the match day, after I've passed through security to enter the stadium, before I find an inconspicuous spot to sit in the stands near the edge of the pitch.

"Well, that part of the plan sounds fool-proof but how will we set about getting the ransom?" asked Frank.

"This is always the most difficult part of the operation if we're to evade capture at the point of delivery," replied Hardman.. "This is where your services will be invaluable. I'll arrange to travel to a nominated underground station where a representative of the club will be waiting to exchange a bag containing the ransom money with a bag containing the FA Cup. We'll have just a few seconds to arrange the swap which involves both parties checking the contents of the bags before the doors close. I fully expect a couple of plain clothes police officers to board the tube at the door, or a door nearby, the point where the bag swap will take place. They'll observe the person who receives the ransom but won't make an arrest until he leaves the train. They can arrest him more easily in the station where people are freely moving than in a crowded underground carriage where they'll have difficulty in even getting near their quarry. I want you to be the one who carries out the swap, Frank!"

"So you've left me with the most risky job. I'll be the fall guy when the arrest is made!" exclaimed Frank.

"Far from it! Calm down," urged Hardman. "You haven't heard the whole plan. I've done the research which will enable you to remain 100% safe. You can be sure that there are many Frank Morris's living in London. I've tracked down several. There's one who lives in central Finchley who's a member of a health club in Highgate. This is important for what comes later. You and I will both get on the tube at 9:15 a.m. at Mill Hill East on the Northern Line and get seat in the last carriage. The worst of the rush hour will be over but the underground will still be very busy. We'll both be carrying identical sports bags bearing the Chelsea Football Club logo. This is important to enable the bags to be readily identified, or misidentified, at crucial points during the change-over. I'll demand that the bag containing the ransom money is also identifiable by bearing the Chelsea FC logo. They are to be ready to swap bags sometime after 9:15 a.m. on East Finchley station with a man carrying a similar bag, in the last carriage which enters the station. The person making the swap (That'll be you) will be standing inside the last door of the underground train carrying a sports bag bearing a Chelsea FC logo. The person bearing the ransom will find you at the arranged door and swap bags. The swap will involve both parties quickly verifying that the bags contain the expected items and, having made the swap, the person who will now have the real FA Cup will not get on this particular train but either leave the station or get on a later train. However, it's almost certain that plain clothes police officers will be observing what goes on and get on the train after the swap has been made. They'll have to be nippy to do this just before the doors close.

Now comes the clever bit. You'll make your way down the carriage to where I'll be sitting. Hopefully, you'll be able to sit next to me but if the train is too crowded, just stand as near to me as you can. You'll leave the train at Highgate, the next stop. However, as you get out, don't pick up the bag containing the money but the bag near me which will contain gym kit of the sort one would wear at a fitness centre. I've discovered that this Frank Morris who lives in Finchley, regularly visits his fitness club in Highgate. As the police follow you off the train, I'll place a Velcro patch over the Chelsea FC logo on the bag in my possession containing the ransom to avoid its being spotted later if anyone else is looking out for a bag sporting this logo."

"This sounds perfect," said Frank as he congratulated Hardman on what appeared to be an intricate but well thought out plan. "I'll just need to clear up a few details of how to deal with the police when they attempt to arrest me at Highgate."

"The police will first demand to see the contents of the bag," explained Hardman. "You can make a mock protest but when they've shown you their warrant cards, you'll let them look into your bag. They'll be surprised to see nothing but gym kit. As they'll be absolutely certain that you're the one they saw make the swap, they won't leave it there. You'll be stealing the identity of someone with the same name as yourself, so you'll easily be able to satisfy the police that you are just about the normal business of going to your health club. I'll get a dummy membership card made out for 'Frank Morris' so that they can phone the health club if they need to check out your story. Dissuade them from phoning your home on the grounds that your wife will have hysterics if she thinks you have been detained by the police. The health club's confirmation of your membership status should provide an adequate identification for the police that you're who you say you are. If they want any more verification, your bank cards or library ticket or any other documentation you have on you will all be in your name of Frank Morris."

Soon after this meeting with Frank, Hardman arranged a meeting in London with the ten lads he'd identified as having close enough resemblances to the Cup Finalists to be accepted as just that by the crowd in the stadium. For the players who were to imitate the Manchester City players, he had bought shirts bearing the names, De Bruyne, Silva, Haaland, Gundogan and Grealish. The corresponding shirts he bought for the Manchester United lookalikes bore the names, Eriksen, Shaw, Sancho, Fernandes and Rashford.

Being Londoners, the young men Hardman had recruited supported teams from their home city, Arsenal, Tottenham Hotspur, Chelsea, Fulham, West Ham United and Crystal Palace. Although normally rivals, the hostilities which existed between supporters of neighbouring clubs like Arsenal and Tottenham, Chelsea and Fulham, were suspended. Instead, they united to focus their wrath on the hated Manchester teams which had done so much damage to London clubs during the season. The young men were delighted to be able to play a part in this particular heist, organised by one with the reputation Hardman bore in the East End of London. Joshua Smith, the blond giant who had been identified as having a good semblance to Erling Haaland, had to be persuaded to grow his blond hair into a pony-tail-cum-bun for the big day Chris Collins who was to be Jack Grealish's double was told that he would need to wear a narrow hairband on the day.

If you are not a football fan, you may prefer to skip the following section in Trebuchet type which explains why supporters of London football clubs felt antagonistic towards the Manchester football clubs. Skipping this will not detract from the story of the heist.

Compared to its London rivals, Fulham is a very small team playing from a modest Thameside ground, Craven Cottage. However, Fulham is a club which punches above its weight standing above its giant neighbour, Chelsea, in the final Premier League table. Fulham had a particular grouse against Manchester United. They were drawn against Fulham in the FA Cup quarter final. During the match, Fulham was dominating the play and had a 1 - 0 lead until the Manchester United players started an uncalled for demonstration to intimidate the referee into awarding them a penalty. This provoked two Fulham players, Willian and Metrovic, and their manager, Marco Silva, to over-react and they were banished by the referee. Playing the rest of the match with only nine men, Fulham inevitably lost the game, 3 – 1.

Premier League 2022/23

	Team	Pl	W	D	L	F	A	GD	Pts
1	Manchester City	38	28	5	5	94	33	61	89
2	Arsenal	38	26	6	6	88	43	45	84
3	Manchester United	38	23	6	9	58	43	15	75
4	Newcastle United	38	19	14	5	68	33	35	71
5	Liverpool	38	19	10	9	75	47	28	67
6	Brighton and Hove Albion	38	18	8	12	72	53	19	62
7	Aston Villa	38	18	7	13	51	46	5	61
8	Tottenham Hotspur	38	18	6	14	70	63	7	60
9	Brentford	38	15	14	9	58	46	12	59
10	Fulham	38	15	7	16	55	53	2	52
11	Crystal Palace	38	11	12	15	40	49	-9	45
12	Chelsea	38	11	11	16	38	47	-9	44
13	Wolverhampton Wanderers	38	11	8	19	31	58	-27	41
14	West Ham United	38	11	7	20	42	55	-13	40
15	Bournemouth	38	11	6	21	37	71	-34	39
16	Nottingham Forest	38	9	11	18	38	68	-30	38
17	Everton	38	8	12	18	34	57	-23	36
18	Leicester City	38	9	7	22	51	68	-17	34
19	Leeds United	38	7	10	21	48	78	-30	31
20	Southampton	38	6	7	25	36	73	-37	25

However, on scrutinising a video of the match, the FA came to the conclusion that the real villains of the piece were not Fulham but Manchester United and fined the club £65,000 for failing to control their players. Thus, the Fulham supporters in the team Hardman had assembled had a very good reason for putting one over the Manchester side.

Arsenal too, were not happy with the Manchester clubs. During the season, Arsenal had dominated the Premier League table, often seven points ahead of their nearest rivals, Manchester City, who were in turn, ten points ahead of the teams in the rest of the table. Even had Arsenal lost to Manchester City in one of the closing matches of the season, they might still have been expected to end the season as Champions, comfortably ahead of their rivals. Then, Arsenal had an end of the season catastrophe in which they drew and lost matches with teams who were well below them in the table. To make matters worse, they had thrown away a two goal lead in two of these matches and failed to convert a penalty which would have given them victory in another of these matches. They went on to lose heavily, 4 – 1, to Manchester City in a key, end-of-the-season match. Had Arsenal won this match, they would have ended the season as champions, one point ahead of Manchester City. In the event, they ended five points behind Manchester City but were still nine points ahead of Manchester

United, the club which ended third in the Premier League final table. They probably still had sad memories of losing to Manchester City, 1 – 0, at the Etihad Stadium in the FA Cup 4th round. This was the first time Arsenal had lost to Manchester City in an FA Cup tie since 1904. Unlike tennis at Wimbledon, the teams playing in the FA Cup are not seeded. Otherwise, it is likely that being so much ahead of other premiership teams, Arsenal and Manchester City would have been seeded to meet in the final. Thus, Arsenal supporters too had reasons to exact revenge against its Manchester rival.

In the final Premier League matches of the season, Manchester City surprisingly lost to Premier League newcomers, Brentford, and Arsenal beat Wolverhampton Wanderers by a thumping 5 – 0, giving them a record for the club of a total of 88 Premier League goals in a season. This total puts into perspective the prolific scoring rate of Manchester City's striker, Erling Haaland who personally scored 38 Premier League goals in the season and a total of over 50 goals for the club if other matches were also taken into account.

With so much money floating around professional football, there are rules to be obeyed off the pitch as well as the laws which control the way the game is played on the field. Clubs must abide by some very strict financial rules. Arsenal will be aware that a four year investigation of Manchester City's finances had revealed over a hundred breaches of financial regulations which could yet lead to a Premier League points reduction for Manchester City. Thus, Arsenal's hopes of being the 2023 champions of the Premier League are not quite dead. English football clubs will be aware of Glasgow Rangers fall from grace as a result of financial irregularities, although this club's going into liquidation is not really comparable to the Manchester City situation.

Other London clubs would also have been smarting after heavy defeats from the Manchester teams, West Ham United losing 3 – 1 to Manchester United in the 5th round of the FA Cup round and Chelsea losing 4– 0 to Manchester City in the 3rd round. Tottenham Hotspur's antagonism to the Manchester teams would have been due to losing 4 – 2 to Manchester City in a Premier League fixture after having had a lead of 2 – 0.

On the day of the Cup Final, things worked out as well as was expected for Hardman. The match started in an absolutely unique way. Their captain, Ilkay Gundogan took the kick-off, straight back to his goalkeeper, Stefan Ortega, who kicked the ball right up the field to where City players had had time to occupy the United half of the pitch. The ball bobbed about as it was headed by two or three players, ending in the path of Gundogan who fired a fierce volley from outside the box, past the left ear of a stunned goalkeeper, De Gea, into the far corner of the United net. This goal, scored with 13 seconds of the kick-off, is a Cup Final record which is unlikely to ever be broken.

De Gea stands stunned after Gundogan's volley
from outside the box opened the scoring.

Later in the match, United equalised with a penalty which was harshly awarded when Grealish was deemed to have handballed, an action which was obviously accidental rather than deliberate. Then in the second half, Gundogan again found the United goal with another fierce volley fired from outside the box so that finally, City ran out 2 – 1 winners.

The Prince of Wales awarded the players and officials their medals and presented the Cup after which the players went onto the pitch to pose for team photographs. Then started the usual parading around the pitch to show off the trophy to their supporters. After these initial celebrations, things started to quieten down. Players were recruited by the BBC to be interviewed on the pitch.

The five Manchester City look-alikes made their way to join their United lookalike colleagues in the rapidly emptying United supporters' part of the stand and passed their tracksuit bottoms to their friends. They were now able to climb over the barrier, looking like City players. The bogus 'Grealish' retrieved the cup from the real Haaland and the bogus 'De Bruyne' retrieved the lid from the real Silva. Hardman had done a good job in selecting his lookalikes. There was not a hint of suspicion that the Cup was being handed to bogus players. The five bogus players moved to surround Hardman who by now had run on to the pitch with his bag. The cups were exchanged without anyone having a clear view or indeed a suspicion of what might be going on. Once the exchange had been completed, Hardman ran out via the players tunnel as if he had just been called on to the pitch to deal with some minor injury. The five bogus players re-joined the genuine players and handed the bogus cup to them to continue their celebrations. They then returned to their colleagues in the stands to put back on their tracksuit bottoms. They all exited the stadium, each £1,000 richer and having enjoyed an exciting Cup Final. There were no security checks on those leaving and Hardman and Frank made their way with the Cup to where Hardman had parked his car.

Hardman contacted the Manchester City management to make them aware that the cup in their possession was only a replica and made arrangements for the real Cup to be exchanged for a ransom.

A few days later, the exchange of the FA cup and the £100,000 ransom was carried out as planned. As expected, on leaving the train, Frank was stopped by two plainclothes police officers who demanded to see the contents of Frank's bag. After initially protesting, Frank allowed the search to be made when the police produced their warrant cards. Discovering nothing but sports kit in Frank's bag, two very puzzled policemen carried out identification checks on Frank but the Health Club and Frank's bank cards all corroborated his story. The police were left wondering what account they were going to give their superiors when being debriefed about what had gone on. Frank proceeded on his way and doubled back to Highgate station when he was well out of view of the police. He caught the underground back to Mill Hill East where Hardman had left his car parked earlier that morning.

They set off for Hardman's home, and a couple of hours later arrived at this largish house which had formerly been a farmhouse. On entering the house, they found Hardman's cleaning lady, Mrs Williams, most of the way through her chores. She offered to make them a cup of tea but they declined, anxious to move on to Frank's house. They first went into Hardman's office where he counted out £5,000, Frank's share of the heist. They stowed this in the sports-bag which was Frank's anyway, and Hardman looked around for a temporary place to store the rest until he could sort it properly. He still had expenses to pay off which had arisen in the course of this enterprise and he would need to make up smaller bundles of notes which he could pay into the various banks where he held accounts, without arousing suspicions of money laundering. He put the rest of the money into a plastic bag he found on the floor near his desk and firmly tied the top so that its contents would not be evident to Mrs Williams, should she have any more cleaning to do in his study.

Hardman quickly got changed and they set off for Frank's home which was within walking distance of an excellent restaurant. They wined and dined, congratulating themselves on a heist well executed. Hardman knew his alcohol limit and drove 'safely' home, late that evening. He parked the car, entered the house by the back door, went up to bed and slept soundly until nearly 10 o'clock the following morning. He got up, had a light breakfast and went into his study to sort out the main share of the ransom money. The plastic bag containing the money wasn't on the desk where he'd left it. He hunted around. No sign of the bag. He phoned Mrs Williams to see if she'd put it anywhere.

"You mean the 'Air Ambulance' charity bag you left on your desk? Yes, I put it out on the front step for collection as I do with all the charity bags which come to the house. 'Air Ambulance' are very efficient and collect these bags quite early. I expect that they will have picked it up by now!"

Manchester City went on to win the European Champions' League Final against Inter Milan, completing an astounding triple of victories, the FA Cup, the Premier League title and the Champions' League Cup, all in one season..

The Tower Ravens

A lasting memory which most visitors will take from a visit to the Tower of London is that of the ravens who contentedly waddle round Tower Green. They will have been told by their guide that should the ravens leave the Tower, disaster will overtake Great Britain and its Commonwealth! The possibility of organising a heist to capture the Tower Ravens and ransom them was the topic of conversation between Richard 'Hardman' Harvey and Frank 'Wheels' Morris.

"I spent last weekend in London," explained Hardman, "visited the Tower and spent sometime with Aaron 'The Vet' Eisenbloom."

"I remember him well," replied Frank. "He used to give us good advice if ever animals were likely to be involved in our escapades but refused to be involved in what I would call the sharp end of our activities. Anyway, he always got a generous cut if ever we benefitted from his advice."

"We certainly pulled off a big one at Newmarket," reminisced Hardman. "Although Charlemagne was a rank outsider, we knew that he was rather better than the bookies gave him credit."

"Yes, he was the second best horse in the Fenland Stakes but we knew he could never beat Arctic Prince."

"That was until we nobbled Arctic Prince with the stuff Aaron had prepared for us and then Charlemagne romped home with three lengths to spare against the long odds of 100-1."

"How's 'The Vet'and why was it you came to look him up?" asked Frank.

"He's fine, still living in the same house in Rotherhithe and carrying on with his vetinerary practice. I looked up Aaron to assess what his reaction might be to an idea I have for carrying out a heist at the Tower of London and to ascertain what professional advice he might be able to give us."

Frank was now all attention.

"A heist at the Tower of London? You're not going to make another attempt at stealing the Crown Jewels?"

"Nothing as ambitious as that," explained Harman. "I thought we might abduct the Tower ravens and ransom them off. You know the legend associated with the Tower ravens. The warning has it that should the ravens leave the Tower, the consequences for Great

Britain are really dire. This means that those running the Tower would pull out all stops to get them back, should the ravens ever go missing."

The Tower of London

"So how do you aim to pull off this one?" asked Frank.

"The information I required from Aaron was how the ravens might be quickly sedated and sent to sleep without their coming to any harm. He gave me some tablets but also a bottle of liquid avian sleeping draught in which we could soak pieces of meat or biscuit which the ravens would snap up. This would send the ravens to sleep within about five minutes but unless they'd eaten lots of pieces of meat or gobbled down an excessive number of pills or biscuits, the effect would only last for about half-an-hour and the birds would wake up.”

“So, if I’ve heard you right, we send these birds off to sleep, gather them up and just walk out of the Tower?” conjectured Frank. “I can’t see that one working.”

“Exactly that, but with a bit of refinement,” explained Hardman. “I’ll enlist the help of three of our East End associates. Harry ‘Keys’ Sullivan, ‘Nobby’ Clark and ‘Nutcase’ Morgan would be ideal for the job. I’ll get T-shirts made up displaying the Royal Coat of Arms and emblazoned ‘Royal Vetinary Service’ for Keys, Nobby and Nutcase. I’ll wear a Yeoman Warder uniform. This has been more difficult to obtain than I’d imagined. There are plenty of the ceremonial bright red, yellow and black uniforms available at theatrical hire outlets. These are in demand from Gilbert and Sullivan Societies performing ‘Yeomen of the Guard’ but I’ll need a black uniform with red piping like the ones the Yeoman Warders wear for everyday use at the Tower. I was finally able to track down one that fitted me at Shepperton Film Studios.”

“I assume that I have a part to play in this?” queried Frank.

"As usual, I want you to drive the getaway car," said Hardman. "I can book a place at the Tower Hill car park in Lower Thames Street which is very near the Tower. Like all London car parks, it's quite expensive, but provided everything goes the way I've planned it, the whole thing will take less than an hour. Keys, Nobby, Nutcase and myself will arrive early and get tickets to enter the Tower. We'll enter the usual way through the Middle and then Byward Towers. However, once in, we won't proceed by the usual route by Traitor's Gate but immediately turn left along what is know as Mint Street and walk right round between the inner and outer walls of the Tower to a tower called Brass Mount. It's unoccupied but locked. However, the large ancient lock shouldn't pose a problem to Keys who can open this kind of lock quite easily using a wire coat hanger.

Brass Mount, Tower of London

1. The White Tower
2. Chapel Royal
3. Waterloo Barracks
4. Fusiliers Headquarters
5. Hospital
6. Workshop
7. Roman City Wall line
8. Wardrobe Tower
9. Inermost Ward wall
10. Coldharbour Gate
11. Scaffold Site
12. Tower Green
13. Queen's House
14. Beauchamp Tower
15. Devereux Tower
16. Flint Tower
17. Bowyer Tower
18. Brick Tower
19. Martin Tower
20. Constable Tower
21. Broad Arrow Tower
22. Salt Tower
23. Lanthorn Tower
24. Wakefield Tower
25. Bloodt Tower
26. Bell Tower
27. Mint Street
28. Casemates
29. Legge's Mount
30. Brass Mount
31. Develin Tower
32. Well Tower
33. Cradle Tower
34. Henry III Watergate
35. St Thomas's Tower
36. Traitor's gate
37. Water Line
38. Byward Tower
39. Middle Tower
40. Lion's Tower
41, Tower Wharf

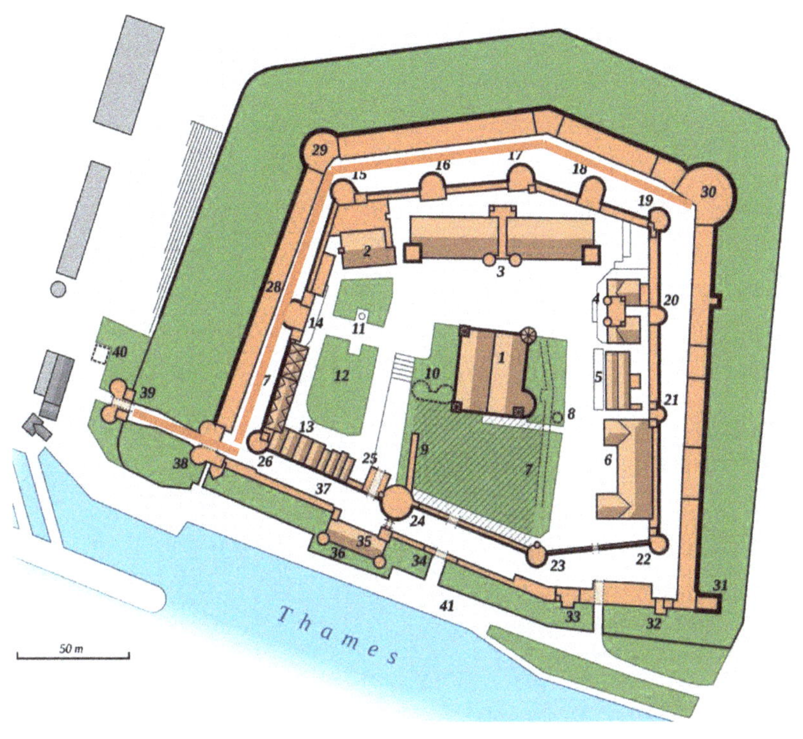

Hardman's route to the Brass Mount

Plan of the Tower of London

We'll do a dry run first however, to ensure this lock doesn't pose an unexpected problem. Once in the Brass Mount, I'll change into the Yeoman Warder's uniform and the others will put on their Royal Vetinary Service T-shirts, clothes which Keys and I will leave in the Brass Mount when we do our dry run.

We'll then make our way back into the main part of the Tower where we'll find the ravens strutting about Tower Green. I'll scatter some of the preprepared raven food. Being in Yeoman Warder uniform, I won't be questioned as I might have been by the Yeoman Warder Raven Master, Chris Skaife, had he been on duty. However, I've discovered he's on leave at the time I plan this heist. The deputy Raven Master is a very new Yeoman and I gather he doesn't really know his way about.

As soon as the ravens fall asleep, Keys, Nobby and Nutcase will carefully place the ravens in two of the sacks we'll be carrying. There are only six ravens. I've discovered that they are called Jubilee, Harris, Poppy, George, Edgar and Branwen. Aaron assures me that provided they're asleep, no harm will come to the ravens if loosely packed, no more than three to a bag.

Tower Raven

We'll make our way back to the Middle and Byward Towers. If obstructed, I'll declare, 'Make way, the ravens have gone down with avian flu and desperately need to be taken to the Royal Vets'. The diversion created by Nobby and Nutcase leaving the Tower will enable Keys and myself to make our way back along Mint Street to the Brass Mount.

The clever part of my plan is that Nobby and Nutcase's bags are just decoys, filled with screwed up paper. Keys and I will be carrying the bags with the real ravens. Once inside the Brass Mount, we'll release the ravens, change back into normal clothes and wait for the ravens to revive. According to Aaron, this should only take a few more minutes. The ravens would only be expected to remain asleep for about half an hour. Once the ravens are awake, we'll depart from the Brass Mount, leaving the ravens locked inside and make our way back and out of the Tower. We'll then proceed to the Tower Hill Car Park where you'll be waiting to drive us to rendezvous with Nobby and Nutcase."

Frank let out a gasp of admiration.

"You seem to have thought this out very well, Hardman. Let's hope it all goes to plan on the day."

"It will," said Hardman, clearly confident that his plan was infallible. "I'm still giving a bit of thought to the way the ransom money may be safely handed over. That's always a problem with this sort of undertaking."

The day of the heist arrived. Hardman left Frank parked in the Tower Hill car park and met Keys, Nobby and

Nutcase as arranged near the Tower. They proceeded to buy tickets and enter the Tower, making their way to the Brass Mount where Hardman and Keys had left the kit they needed to wear, on the dry run they'd carried out earlier. Thus attired as a Yeoman Warder and as Royal Vets, and carrying the bags they would need, they made their way back to the main part of the Tower where Hardman spread the doctored raven food he had brought, near to the ravens on Tower Green after making sure that the deputy Raven Master was not in view.

Hardman feeds a Tower Raven

The food worked as Aaron had predicted. As soon as the sixth raven had roosted, Hardman and his associates loaded the sleeping ravens into their bags. By this time, the deputy Raven Master was aware that something untoward was going on with his ravens.

"What are you doing?" he yelled as he rushed to the Green.

"These birds have got Avian flu," shouted Hardman. "We've got to get them to the vets as soon as possible."

"Then I'm coming too," replied the deputy Raven Master. He assumed that Hardman was a senior Yeoman Warder he hadn't previously met.

In the panic that ensues an unpredictable event like this, the illogicality of vets being immediately on call to rescue the apparently stricken ravens as soon as they were seen to be ill, was a thought the deputy Raven Master couldn't immediately process. He assumed that the disguised Hardman, as a senior Yeoman Warder, had everything under control. His concern was to be with his ravens and this suited Harman and company well. They made their way to the Byward Tower and then the Middle Tower crying 'Make Way!', 'Emergency!' Seeing three men wearing clothing which seemed to indicate that they were vets, accompanied by two Yeoman Warders, one of whom they reognised as the deputy Raven Master, meant that the officers on duty at the gate offered no obstruction to the fleeing group. The main attention was focused on the deputy Raven Master, and Nobby and Nutcase, carrying bags of apparent importance but in reality, stuffed with paper. They proceeded to the Middle Tower and out to a waiting taxi. The three of them got in the taxi which drove to Bethnal Green where Nobby and Nutcase alighted and paid the cabby to return to the Tower with the Yeoman Warder. As soon as the taxi set off, the deputy Raven Master looked in the bags Nobby and Nutcase had left, expecting to find his precious ravens. He was astonished to find no more than tightly screwed up paper.

Earlier, at the Tower, with the main attention thus diverted to the trio leaving the Tower and entering the taxi, Hardman and Keys made their way down Mint Street to the Brass Mount and once inside, they took the ravens out of their bags. Luckily, they were still peacefully asleep. Hardman and Keys changed back into normal clothes and waited for the ravens to revive. True to Aaron's word, the ravens were all up, awake and strutting about within half-an-hour of their abduction. Hardman scattered a load of uncontaminated bits of meat around the Brass Mount floor and Hardman and Keys made their way out, leaving the ravens, slightly disorientated by their new environment but happily gobbling up the titbits left for them. Hardman and Keys calmly departed from the

Tower and made their way to the Tower Hill carpark where Frank was waiting for them. On his way out, Hardman had left an envelope with the guard on duty marked 'URGENT' and addressed to the Constable of the Tower, Sir Nick Houghton. He stressed that this should be delivered as soon as possible. It contained information about the ravens.

Once back at the car, Hardman left Keys with Frank and made his way to nearby Hart Street. In case the envelope he had left hadn't been delivered to the Constable, he phoned the Tower and asked to be put in touch with the Constable of the Tower. The Constable wasn't in residence at the time but the call was taken by Simon Mayall who, as Lieutenant of the Tower, was the Constable's deputy.

"Your ravens are well and will be returned safely if a ransom of £5,000 is paid," explained Hardman. "The ransom must be delivered to me at 5:00 p.m. where I will be standing outside 'The Ship Inn' in Hart Street. I'll then phone you to let you know how to recover the ravens. You can allow the bearer to release the cash to me when you are satisfied that the ravens are safely back in your possession. If there is any sign of police involvement in this drop off, the ravens are dead!"

The message was received and understood.

Frantic activity now ensued. The Lieutenant ascertained that £5,000 could be provided from the day's takings and bundles of £500 were made up and labelled from the money collected from the Tower tills. Indeed, with so many people paying by credit card, accumulating £5,000 in notes stretched the Tower's accessible liquid cash resources to the limit.

By coincidence, Detective Inspector Christine Powers was in the Tower when all this was going on. She was on leave and spending a few days sightseeing while staying with her elderly aunt in London. Being aware of the commotion on Tower Green, she made her way to the Constable's House, introduced herself as a senior police officer and showed her warrant card.

"What's happening? Can I be of help?" she asked.

She was shown into a room in the house where the Lieutenant of the Tower was frantically counting out money with the help of three assistants. He was glad to have a senior police officer present and appraised her of what was happening.

"The legend states that if the ravens leave the Tower, calamity will overcome Great Britain and the Commonwealth," Simon Mayall explained. "This could become a self-fulfilling prophecy if it produces a negative reaction among enough people who believe the legend. Sadly, the conditions laid down for paying the ransom mean that the police can't be overtly involved but you may be able to give helpful advice."

"For my own protection, I always carry a GPS (Global Positionaing System) chip," stated Christine. "Might I suggest that you sow this chip into the bag which will contain the money you will be passing on to the ransomers."

The Lieutenant's face became slightly less clouded at this suggestion.

"What a good idea. We'll at least be able to track the money which will help in its recovery."

Christine gave the Lieutenant her GPS chip which he gratefully accepted. He gave it to an assistant to sow into the bag in which the the ransom money was being loaded. She cleverly sewed in the chip in a such a way that the it would remain inconspicuous.

Christine phoned back to her Chief Inspector, Colin Whittaker, in Oakenhampton who in turn contacted the Met. By now, the Tower had alerted the Met to the situation but the Met couldn't do much in view of the threat included in the ransom demand. However, they sent a police officer to the Tower to be avaible if there was any help he could give.

A senior Yeoman Warder dressed in civvies was sent to Hart Street with the ransom. He identified Hardman waiting outside 'The Ship'. The Yeoman Warder opened the bag to enable Hardman to see the notes inside without letting go of the bag. Hardman then phoned back to the Tower and his call was picked up by Simon Mayall, the Lieutenant of the Tower.

"You'll find the ravens safe and well in the Brass Mount. If I don't hear back from you in ten minutes, enabling your man to hand me the ransom, my men will come and forcibly take it from him," Hardman bluffed.

Within ten minutes, the Yeoman Warder's phone rang, informing him that the ravens were safe. He handed over the bag to Hardman who swiftly departed, apparently going towards Tower Hill underground station. However, he actually went to the car park where Frank and Keys were waiting and they drove off to a rendezvous he had arranged with Nobby and Nutcase.

They arrived at the Sun Tavern in Bethnal Green Road where Nobby and Nutcase were already waiting and after ordering a round of drinks, they sat in a secluded alcove where they shared out the money. This didn't take long as the notes had already been sorted in the Tower into bundles of £500. They shared £1,000 each and after congratulations all round at a job successfully pulled off, they quickly departed after quaffing their drinks. As experienced criminals on a job, they knew that it didn't pay to stick around together in one place. They left the empty ransom bag in the pub.

By now, the police had picked up the signal from Christine's GPS and descended on the Sun Tavern where they recovered the bag but found their quarry had departed. They obtained as good a description of the men involved as possible but this was a busy time for the pub and the information given was fairly sketchy.

Things now began to settle down again at the Tower. The Lieutenant and warders, especially the deputy Raven Master, could breathe sighs of relief as the totally unconcerned but precious ravens again roamed their familiar environment. Technically, they'd never left the Tower but had only been temporarily displaced to a different environment in the Brass Mount which lay within the Tower complex.

On return to duty after completing her leave, Christine discussed what had happened in the Tower with her Chief Inspector.

"The Met say that they've nothing to go on to enable them to investigate this case except a vague description of the men involved," said Colin Whittaker.

"That's not entirely true," said Christine. "For a start, the ringleader was wearing the everyday uniform of a Yeoman Warder. Where did he get this? There's no report of a uniform being stolen from the Tower."

"He must have hired it from a theatrical agency or fancy dress hire shop," said Colin. "This must be a very common form of fancy dress or theatre clothing to hire."

"Not really," countered Christine. "The normal Yeoman Warder uniform which will be on demad for hire will be the spectacular, red, yellow and black uniforms. Gilbert and Sullivan societies in particular will need these if they put on the operetta, 'Yeoman of the Guard'. No, the everyday Yeoman Warder uniform they wear on normal duty won't be in great demand. I'll arrange for our Detective Sergeant, Bill Matthews, to trail through fancy dress hire agencies to see if there's a record of such an item being out on hire during the week the ravens were abducted. I think that a film studio rather than a theatrical agency or fancy dress shop might have such costumes available."

Christine was absolutely right. Pinewood Studios in Shepperton did have such costumes which they'd bought from the Tower of London as second hand clothing some years earlier. This had been needed for the extras taking part in what we would call a B movie which was partly filmed within the Tower of London, and yes, a Yeoman Warder costume had been out on loan during that particular week to one, Richard Harvey.

The following day, Christine and Bill made their way to the Pinewood Studios in Shepperton to get documentary evidence of this hiring taking place. This would be needed in court, should Hardman ever be brought to trial for kidnapping the ravens. The charge would be for extortion rather than kidnapping a few birds, special though they may have been.

"I don't think this evidence will be quite enough to secure a conviction," said Colin Whittaker, "but now we know it's Hardman, we can surely dig up some more evidence."

"That we can," Christine triumphantly suggested. "We know the registration number of Hardman's car. We can examine the footage on London surveillance camera's for the date of the theft to see if Hardman's car was there. With the extra cameras installed in London to enable congestion charges to be levied, we should find Harvey's car appearing on one or other of the cameras if it was there."

Detective Sergeant Bill Matthews was given the job of examining the traffic surveillance cameras and as the time span in question was fairly narrow, it didn't take too long to carry out this task. Yes, Hardman's car was picked up around the Tower of London on that date and indeed, the camera footages enabled Hardman's car to be tracked both into London and out again on the day of the theft, all the way from and back to the Cotswolds. It was with great satisfaction the Christine and Bill arrived at Hardman's house with the arrest warrant.

"Richard Harvey, I am arresting you on suspicion of an act of extortion, carried out against the Tower of London, You do not have to say anything, but it may harm your defence if you do not mention when questioned, something that you rely on in court. Anything you do say may be given in evidence."

In due course, Hardman was tried. It took a while for the jury to agree on a verdict but at last, they were all convinced that Hardman (Richard Harvey) was guilty. When his previous criminal record was disclosed, they all felt confident that they'd come to the right decision. Hardman couldn't restore the ransom money because it had already been shared out and true to the criminal class code, he wasn't about to 'grass' on his accomplices. Colin Whittaker contacted the RSPCA to see if there was any chance of getting a 'cruelty to animals' charge levelled against Hardman but as the ravens had been returned in good spirits and unharmed, he wasn't able to use this to get Hardman's sentence increased. However, in view of his criminal record, Hardman was given the heaviest sentence possible for this crime.

Christine, Bill and Colin felt a deep sense of satisfaction that their nemesis, who had so frequently evaded justice when being investigated for crimes committed on their patch, would at last be put behind bars. The Oakenhampton team, and Christine in particular, received a commendation for the part they had played in solving this crime .

The Magna Cartas

Richard 'Hardman' Harvey and Frank 'Wheels' Morris were enjoying a pint of beer at the Black Greyhound, a well-appointed pub just down the road from where Frank lived. As usual, their conversation turned to what might be their next big enterprise. It was invariably Hardman who came up with the most ambitious ideas. The recent ventures aimed at high profile targets had been so well organised that they were invariably successful up to a point. Some snag usually arose right at the end of the enterprise when the pair were beginning to congratulate themselves on their success. Then something happened which prevented their enjoying their ill-gotten gains.

"There are only four original copies of the Magna Carta still in existence," Hardman informed Frank. "Two are in the British Library in London, the best preserved is in Salisbury Cathedral and Lincoln Cathedral is custodian of the other which is stored in Lincoln Castle. I think we could get the cathedrals concerned to pay a ransom if their copies of the Magna Carta were to suddenly disappear," suggested Harman. "I think we could demand £5,000 for each of the Magna Carta's safe return."

Salisbury Cathedral

"There would be big problems in attempting that," countered Frank, "Not least in getting them out, past security at the cathedral entrance."

"That wouldn't be a significant obstacle in the plan I've devised," Hardman replied. "Bear in mind that it's not the actual Magna Carta we need but the ransom which would be paid for a missing Magna Carta to be recovered. I've been to examine the way the document is stored at both the cathedrals which hold copies. In each case, the Magna Carta is contained in a glass fronted frame. When the attention of the tourists who were with me was diverted, I quickly measured the dimensions of these frames and took a photograph. If anyone saw me do this, they weren't unduly concerned. They certainly didn't report me to cathedral security staff who might have wondered what I was up to."

Magna Carta in Salisbury Cathedral

"What do you hope to do with this information?" queried Frank.

"I will make up two frames, containing facsimiles of the original document, identical to the ones in Salisbury Cathedral and Lincoln Castle" explained Hardman. "Excellent copies of the Magna Carta can be obtained at very reasonable prices. Pitkins sell them for £2.65 and they can be obtained on Ebay for £4.32. The Ebay copy may be of slightly higher quality. If stored within a glazed frame, they couldn't be touched or felt to discover that they were prepared on paper rather than vellum."

"And just how would these framed copies of the Magna Carta be used?"

"They would simply be placed on top of and fixed to the original frames. Unless one was actually looking to see if this had been done, the fact that the document on display was two centimetres nearer than when usually viewed just wouldn't be noticed."

Everything was now clear to Frank who could see that different challenges now had to be met.

"So the problem would not be in carrying the Magna Carta out of the cathedral or castle but in smuggling the bogus copy in," concluded Frank. "And then, how are you going to fit the bogus frames on top of the genuine article without being seen. This will be a much more difficult thing to do than just making two measurements or taking a photograph"

"I have contacted the cathedral authorities, describing myself as an artist who would like to paint pictures of the interior of their cathedral or castle and requesting written permission to bring into the cathedral my artist's bag. This will contain blank canvasses, paints, tools like brushes and an easel. The bag would also contain the frame to be fixed over the original Magna Carta frame. The glass will be covered with a peel off picture to conceal what the frame really contains from anyone wishing to check the contents of my artist's bag. One of the tools will be an impact driver which can be used to insert panel pins with the pressure of the hand rather than using something noisy like a hammer. The frame could be initially held in position using something like blue tack but that wouldn't be durable enough to last the period of the heist. Once positioned, the frame will need to be secured by panel pins, preferably driven in from beneath through the original frame rather than from above. However, if there seems to be too much time pressure, the pins may be driven in from the top of the frame as this would be an easier way to get the job done."

"My word," said an admiring Frank, "You've taken important steps in getting this heist planned, but I still think there'll be a problem in securing the bogus document frame over the genuine article without being noticed."

"You're quite right. Although it will only take a couple of minutes, this is too long to complete the job unobserved unless a diversion can be created to keep everyone's attention away from the Magna Carta display."

"You usually require my help to carry out this sort of venture," said Frank, "but I can't see what part I might play!"

"I rather think that I might be better at creating a diversion than you," said Hardman "but you're very good with your hands, doing practical things. I would want you to be the artist, which will involve the task of fitting the bogus frame over the original Magna Carta. You would go into the cathedral or castle ahead of me, get set up near the Magna Carta and start painting. When I come in and create the diversion, that will be the sign for you to install the bogus frame."

So it was, Frank found himself bearing his artist's bag and entering Salisbury Cathedral early one Spring morning. He showed the security staff at the entrance, the letter Hardman had received from the Dean and Chapter explaining why he should be admitted, carrying an artist's bag.

It took Frank a little while to locate the Magna Carta in the Chapter House but he soon set up his easel and canvass nearby and started to paint a picture of the interior of the Chapter House. There were about a dozen or so tourists ambling around, some showing more interest in Frank's painting than the Magna Carta on display.

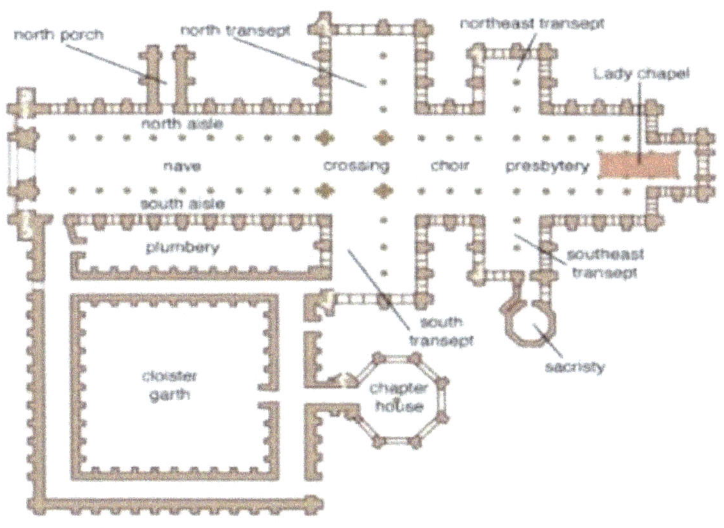

Salisbury Cathedral Ground Plan

Salisbury Cathedral Chapter House

About half-an-hour later, Hardman arrived. It was his job to create a diversion which would take people's attention away from the Magna Carta and any activity that Frank might undertake in association this heist. Hardman had come well prepared. He wore a prominent badge proclaiming :-

**'HISTORY & CULTURE
CAMPAIGNS
SALISBURY INITIATIVE'**

He had a number of blank sheets on which an octagon had been marked, filling the page. This octagon represented the outline of the Chapter House and an arrow showed north. The position of the door on the west wall was marked. Standing on the ledge, on the opposite side of the Chapter House to where Frank was ostensibly painting the Chapter House interior, Hardman spoke out in a clear voice,

"The Cathedral staff think that English people don't know their Bibles," he declared, "so I want to prove them wrong. The sculptured figures set in the arcading around the Chapter House wall represent incidents which occurred in the Old Testament. I have written down a list of some of the incidents included and I want you to mark on the octagon blanks I am giving you, the description of the incident against which of the eight walls the incident is displayed. You should find one for each wall, but two for the west wall, one each side of the door. Come and collect your sheets and start now. Families are allowed to work together. There are no prizes but include your name and age when you give your completed octagon answer sheets to me."

During the time that Hardman had been speaking and the tourists' attention directed away from himself, Frank had taken the bogus Magna Carta frame from his bag and fixed it over the genuine frame.

Sculptures in arcading of Salisbury
Cathedral Chapter House

He peeled off the picture on the glass which was there to conceal the bogus Magna Carta. By the time the tourists started to pay attention to the sculptures set in the Chapter House walls, to fill in the octagons on their answer sheets, Frank was already back at his easel, busy with his paint brush. During the time that Hardman had addressed the tourists, they were all standing with their backs to Frank, and in any case, no-one would suspect that anything untoward was going on in full sight of Hardman who seemed to have an official position in the cathedral.

(For the interest of any who are likely to be visiting Salisbury Cathedral in the not too distant future, the Old Testament incidents which Hardman had included and the wall where they appeared were as follows. To give the activity the flavour of a quiz, Hardman hadn't put them in the order below.

W   The Creation
NW   Adam and Eve hiding
N   Cain slaying Abel
NE   Building the Tower of Babel
E   Jacob and the angels
SE   Joseph thrown into the well
S   Joseph's cup placed in Benjamin's sack
SW   Pharaoh's army destroyed in the Red Sea.
W   Moses receiving the tablets of stone)

Once Hardman had finished distributing all the octagon blanks and the list of Old Testament incidents he had brought along, he came over to where Frank was still busy painting, cast his eye over the canvass and then went on to inspect the Magna Carta. Frank had done a good job in securing the frame containing the bogus Magna Carta. One would have had no idea that there was another frame under the top display frame. Hardman felt the top frame. It had been securely fixed and the panel pins, which Frank must have impacted in from below, were not visible from above.

At midday, Frank packed away the painting kit and was joined by Hardman as they went to the Cathedral refectory for a spot of lunch.

Lincoln Cathedral

The following day, the couple made their way to Lincoln where they carried out a similar charade. This time, the Magna Carta was to be found in the David Ross Vault in Lincoln Castle. Hardman had to use a different distraction technique. There were fewer tourists in the vault than there had been in Salisbury Cathedral Chapter House but they seemed to be well informed.

Again, standing at an elevated vantage point in the vault but well away from Frank, Hardman challenged the tourists,

Lincoln Castle

Magna Carta in Lincoln Castle

157

"How many of you think that the Wars of the Roses should have been won by the Yorkists and how many of you are glad that ultimately, the Lancastrians prevailed?" he challenged.

The tourists were split, roughly 50:50.

"Do you Yorkist supporters consider that a descendant of the Earl of Lincoln, who was killed at the Battle of Stoke Field, the last conflict in the Wars of the Roses, should be king now? After all, he was nominated by King Richard III to be his successor."

Some of those present who were citizens of Lincoln and who had claimed to support the Lancastrian succession, had not considered that perhaps their own Earl had a right to the throne, and they changed their allegiance."

A Lancastrian supporter spoke out.

"Of course he shouldn't. The first Yorkist king, Edward IV, had no claim to the throne because in reality, he was an illegitimate son of the Duke of York. Documentary evidence shows that his mother, Cecily Neville, conceived him at a time when the Duke of York was nowhere near her but away, fighting in another part of France."

A Yorkist supporter then spoke up.

"Even if that were true, the Earl of Lincoln, John de la Pole's mother, Elizabeth, was the legitimate daughter of Richard, Duke of York. The one whose claim is in doubt is Henry Tudor, for he was the descendant of John Beaufort, the illegitimate son of John of Gaunt, Duke of Lancaster, and Katharine Swynford,"

Another voice came up from a Lancastrian supporter.

John of Gaunt and Katharine Swynford did get married and their previous children were legitimised by a charter of King Richard II"

This sort of argument was just what Hardman and Frank had wanted for it diverted attention from Frank as he fixed the bogus framed Magna Carta on top of the genuine one, much as he had done so at Salisbury Cathedral.

Later, that evening, Hardman and Frank had returned home and were discussing the next phase of the operation, 'how to secure the ransom money'.

"This is always the most difficult task," declared Hardman. "Securing the object to be ransomed carries the element of surprise but once the conditions for handing over the ransom have been agreed, the authorities can put plans into motion to retrieve the money, once it has been handed over."

"So, what plans have you in mind?" asked Frank.

"I'll write to the Deans of Salisbury and Lincoln Cathedrals, letting them know that the copies of Magna Carta on display are fake. They will discover this is the case when they look at the documents on display and discover a small red crown has been marked on the bottom, right hand corner. I'll dissuade them from removing the fake documents until the real documents have been returned, both in the interest of the viewing public and the cathedral's reputation for security. The location of the real documents will be revealed when I receive a ransom of £5,000 from each cathedral. This is to be delivered to me at Euston Station where I will be found, standing near the Arrivals & Departures Display Board, wearing a conspicuous red cap and carrying a sports bag, bearing the Chelsea Football Club logo.

Once the cathedral representatives have rendezvoused with me and I have ascertained that the money is as required, I will pass the sports bag over to them to transfer the money to this bag. We'll then make our way to Slasher's Left Luggage facility near the station where the cathedral's representatives may leave the sports bag in a numbered locker. They will retain the key until the cathedral authorities are satisfied that the Magna Carta documents are safe and in the cathedrals' possession. I will return to Euston Station with them whence they can phone the cathedrals and I will let them know where the Magna Cartas are to be found. As soon as the cathedrals have the Magna Cartas, their representatives are to hand me the left luggage facility key. No violence will be involved if these instructions are carried out to the letter. I will lead them to believe that any sign of police involvement will result in the destruction of the Magna Cartas."

"Well, that sounds clear enough," said Frank, "but we can be fairly sure that plain clothes officers will be watching out and move in to arrest you as soon as they are informed that the documents are safe."

"This is where you will have a part to play Frank. Before I meet up with the cathedrals' representatives, you are to deposit at Slasher's Left Luggage facility, a sports bag, bearing the Chelsea Football Club logo, identical to the one in which the ransom money is to be held. However, this bag will contain no more than old books. You will have the numbered key to the locker in which your bag has been deposited. The station will be pretty crowded at this time and in these crowded conditions, it will be possible for us to get close enough to swap locker keys in a way which will not be observed by any police following me on the crowded concourse. I will dump my red cap but I think the police will keep me in sight until I have retrieved the bag, that'll be your bag of books. They won't move in to arrest me until I move off with the bag and then, they'll discover that I'm not absconding with the ransom money. This is similar to the ruse we used to divert the police's attention from the ransom money paid to retrieve the FA Cup.

Soon after I've left the Left Luggage Facility, you're to use the key I have given you to retrieve the bag containing the money. It'll be advisable to cover the Chelsea football club logo with a Velcro patch which I'll give you. Make your way to Marylebone station and take a train to Warwick Parkway where we left my car parked this morning. I'll meet you there if we don't bump into each other on the train."

The ransom handover proceeded even more smoothly than expected. Hardman was met by two minor canons from their respective cathedrals, carrying the ransom money. Once they had locked the ransom money in a box at Slasher's Left Luggage facility and returned to Euston station, they phoned their cathedrals. On hearing back that the Magna Cartas were safe, they handed Harman the Left Luggage box key and returned to their home cities. Hardman was not stopped by plain clothes police officers whom he had expected to have been briefed on how to recover the ransom money. Indeed, at that stage, neither Salisbury nor Lincoln Cathedral authorities had informed the police of the missing Magna Cartas for fear that an over enthusiastic police constable might act prematurely and jeopardise the safety of these irreplaceable documents. Once they had discovered that their genuine copies of the Magna Carta were unharmed, they contacted their local police headquarters. While they wanted these crimes investigated, they wanted no publicity whatever. Any publicity would undermine the general public's confidence in the ability of a body like a cathedral to safeguard priceless national treasures and would be bad for the cathedrals' reputation.

Hardman and Frank met up on the train to Warwick Parkway and that evening, they relaxed as they counted out and shared the money, proud to have pulled off another successful heist. Little did they realise that they weren't quite out of the wood yet.

At Oakenhampton Police Station, Detective Inspector Christine Powers and Detective Sergeant Bill Matthews were browsing through documents which get circulated around police headquarters, outlining unsolved crimes which had been committed in other areas of the country. They were intrigued to discover a pair of copycat crimes committed against the cathedrals of Salisbury and Lincoln, the ransoming of stolen copies of the Magna Carta. Christine and Bill simultaneously came up with two suspects.

"These crimes bear the hallmark of Richard Harvey and Frank Morris," declared Christine.

"These were the very names I'd come up with in my mind," agreed Bill.

With the permission of their Chief Inspector, Colin Whittaker, they got in touch with the Wiltshire Police and Lincolnshire Constabulary who provided them with enough information to start an investigation. This proved relatively easy as they already had their suspects in mind. Pictures they could recognise as Richard Harvey and Frank Morris showed up on the closed circuit TV security cameras in both the cathedrals, Frank carrying his bag of 'artists' materials'. Richard 'Hardman' Harvey was clearly seen, standing near the Arrivals and Departures Screen on Euston Station wearing a red cap and talking to two clerics. The absence of close circuit TV sightings on traffic surveillance cameras of Richard Harvey's car around Euston and out of London suggested that the couple had left London by public transport. Examination of CCTV pictures at West London rail termini revealed both Hardman and Frank, carrying sports bags, boarding a train at Marylebone, and yes, Hardman's car was picked up leaving Warwick Parkway station. They enquired of the Wiltshire and Lincolnshire police if fingerprints and DNA samples had been taken from the cases which housed the Magna Cartas. Yes, but there were so many that examining all the data available and comparing it to the national criminal database record without any suspects in mind would have resulted in overload of police energy and available computer time. Once, two possible suspects with criminal records were suggested, the fingerprint and DNA evidence was re-examined. Yes, a match was found with the fingerprints and DNA of Frank Morris.

With this evidence, the police felt that they could go ahead and make arrests. However, the cathedral authorities didn't want a leak to lead to any publicity and requested that the police should proceed no further but let the cathedrals know the names of the suspects. This was irregular but a body like a cathedral, shunning adverse publicity, would be unlikely to misuse this information. They deserved any help the police could give to recover their losses, even though the manner in which this was done might be unorthodox.

A high power meeting was arranged between the cathedral authorities of Salisbury and Lincoln which included both Bishops and Deans. The Right Reverend Stephen Lake, Bishop of Salisbury, and the Right Reverend Stephen Conway, Bishop of Lincoln, didn't conform to the stereotypical image of a bishop being a very straight faced individual with no sense of humour.

"I think we can breathe a sigh of relief," started Bishop Stephen Lake, "now that we know that the original Magna Cartas are in our possession and indeed, never actually left our possession. I commend the ransomers on their ingenuity but not on their morals. I've had a chat with my fellow bishop and I think we can make sure that the ransom money is put to proper use without actually involving the police who've been able to identify for us the names of those involved in the heist."

"Yes," said Bishop Stephen Conway. "We've ascertained that the £5,000 paid by each cathedral could be regarded as part of the cathedrals' budgeted money for giving to charity. Provided the money actually gets to the nominated charities, it doesn't matter too much that the cheques they receive won't bear the cathedral stamp. We'll write to the charities we support, asking them to send requests for donations to their charities to Richard Harvey and Frank Morris whose names and addresses we'll provide. These are the two individuals who received the ransom money. Far better that the church should do this to give the perpetuators of a crime the opportunity for restitution rather than proceed with an act of vengeance!"

Bishop Stephen Lake continued.

"We'll send these gentlemen letters under our signatures which we think will induce them to contribute to the nominated charities, the money they have taken from us. We'll only involve the police as a last resort if our stratagem doesn't work."

The following is a copy of the letter which was sent to the addresses of both Hardman and Frank.

South Canonry, Salisbury
13, Eastgate, Lincoln

August 2023

Dear Mr. Harvey and Mr. Morris,

While we admire your ingenuity in obtaining the money you demanded before you would reveal where you had concealed our copies of the Magna Carta, we cannot commend such dishonesty. However, your actions have done no great damage to the Magna Cartas or to our cathedrals. On the contrary, our tax liability has been lessened and we may be able to claim on our insurance. However, we would not want to make such a claim and this will not be necessary if you can help us dispose of the money, of which you have become custodians, in a manner which befits the purposes for which the money was originally donated.

We have asked those who would normally receive charitable donations direct from our cathedrals, to send their requests for support to you. Do study the information these bodies will send to you so that you may realise how the money will be used to protect children in the developing world from going blind, to provide clean water for those subject to contracting disease from their currently available polluted water supplies, to provide relief and healing from debilitating diseases like leprosy and malaria and to provide schooling and education for those who might otherwise remain illiterate. Request that these charities send you receipts for any donations they receive and forward on these receipts to ourselves, care of our respective cathedrals.

You may wonder how we come to know your identities. You left a trail of evidence in the form of fingerprints and DNA in the cathedral and castle, images on CCTV in these buildings, at London main line terminals and at Warwick Parkway. You were seen to drive your car from Warwick Parkway after the elapse of a train journey's time, following on from your being observed at Marylebone. With this evidence, the police are anxious to proceed with a prosecution. However, we have urged them not to do so until we have had a chance to make what we consider to be a better arrangement. Should you exercise a satisfactory stewardship of the money which has passed from our responsibility to yours, no prosecution will take place. We suggest that individual cheques are made out to no more than £100 at a time, making further donations as you receive repeat requests. However, we await viewing copies of the receipts from the charities to *which you will have hopefully responded before we make a final decision on involving the police.*

We remain committed servants of our Lord and pastoral carers for those whose souls are our responsibility.

Stephen Lake,   **Stephen Conway,**
Bishop of Salisbury,   **Bishop of Lincoln**

Hardman and Frank were dismayed to receive these letters and met up to discuss their response.

"If we wish to escape prosecution." said Hardman, "I don't see that we have any alternative but to follow the Bishops' request to the letter".

Frank reluctantly agreed.

The next few months found Hardman and Frank writing cheques to the numerous charities which the cathedrals supported. This task was an important educational experience for Hardman and Frank, for as they read the information which came with the requests, they became aware as never before of the extent of suffering and misery of so many people living in the less developed parts of the world. They kept a tally of the sums of money they were paying out.

After the cathedrals had received receipts showing that Hardman and Frank had paid out a cumulative total of at least £10,000 to the charities they had nominated, they sent Hardman and Frank letters saying that any intention on the cathedrals' part to proceed with prosecution had been dropped.

<u>The Fire</u>

Richard 'Hardman' Harvey and Frank 'Wheels' Morris were reminiscing over recent events which had taken place in their lives. Among these were heists aimed at very high profile targets.

"Our recent enterprises haven't turned out as well they might," lamented Harvey, "but in spite of that, I feel a change has come over me, directing me to look at life from a totally different standpoint."

"Strangely, I feel much the same," added Frank "and I very much think that this has been the result of the way our attempt to ransom the Magna Cartas turned out."

"The only heist which brought us in any financial profit," mused Hardman, "was the theft of Canterbury Cathedral's processional cross which we sold to an American Museum, prepared to display it and make claims which they certainly couldn't justify. The fact that they could also display a press cutting indicating that it had been stolen was used to boost if not to fully authenticate their claim. They put this cross in the same category as the Elgin Marbles displayed in the British Museum which many think were stolen."

"Yes, I think those bright cops from the Thames Valley Constabulary were hot on our tails and we only escaped because the Cathedral didn't want to press charges."

"I think we did really well to steal St Edward's Crown," continued Hardman, "causing the authorities to run the coronation with a substitute crown. Sadly, the money we received had been doctored to be traceable but, in a sense, we had the last laugh. We escaped being prosecuted because revelation of our crime would have caused too much embarrassment for many in high places."

"Sadly, the expenses we incurred were not recoverable," reflected Frank. "The replica crown cost a lot of money and the case I had made to accommodate the real crown didn't come cheap."

"Stealing the Irish Guards mascot was a lot of fun," added Hardman. "To avoid disappointing you, I didn't tell you what went wrong at the end. Fortunately, you already had your share of the money, but a group of Irish guardsmen somehow found out where I lived and I had to give them back my share and more to avoid their damaging my car. Because I couldn't quite return all that they demanded, they smashed one of my windows and I had to get this repaired."

Frank hadn't been told of this but remained silent to avoid causing Hardman the embarrassment which further probing would have induced.

"The enterprise which gives me most pride," said Hardman "was taking the FA Cup in full sight of the crowd at Wembley. Sadly, my stupid housekeeper left the bag containing the money out for the Air Ambulance charity to collect. My fault for not checking that the plastic bag I used to temporarily store the money wasn't a charity bag."

"In view of our most recent experience in which the money we secured was paid out to charities," added Frank, "I'm pleased in a way that that money went to a really worthwhile charity. It may well have helped Air Ambulance to save lives. At least the football clubs with their obscene wealth won't really have missed the money."

"I thought that ransoming the Tower ravens worked really well," mused Hardman, "but we hadn't taken into account the over-zealous Thames Valley police and I recouped a prison sentence. Fortunately, I got out early on the basis of being well behaved. I'm glad that at least our East London colleagues who helped us with that, did get recompensed with their share of the takings."

"The Magna Carta heist worked well to a point," added Frank. "I realise now how shrewd the cathedral authorities were in allowing us the responsibility of allocating the cash to the charitable causes to which the cathedrals would have otherwise paid out directly themselves. I learnt so much in reading about the plight of people living in so many in developing countries. The pictures shown of the happy faces, both of those who had been helped and those charity workers who supported these desperate people, made me wish that I had spent my life doing something like this rather than living a life of crime which has barely brought us any profit."

"You're right, Frank," was Hardman's rueful answer, "but what can we do at this late stage in our lives to make amends? Our lifestyle so alienated our wives that our marriages failed, our friends are hardly the best people in the world and we've criminal records a mile long!"

"The attitude shown by the Bishops of Salisbury and Lincoln leaves me feeling that joining a church wouldn't be a bad idea," suggested Frank.

"Would any church be prepared to accept a couple like us?" mused Hardman. "We're hardly what might be called pillars of society."

"We live well out in the sticks some distance from any town," countered Frank. "If we joined a church, no-one would know anything about us. If we find we don't fit in, we can just leave. Our nearest town is Oakenhampton. Whenever I've been there on a Sunday morning to buy a newspaper, I've always been impressed at the generally happy expressions on the faces of those leaving St Giles. Let's try there next Sunday."

St Giles, Oakenhampton

So it was, the following Sunday found Hardman and Frank in their best clothes making their way to St Giles for the 11:00 a.m. morning service. They didn't know what to expect and were favourably impressed by the lively singing and enthusiastic worship. The Vicar's talk held their interest too. They were invited to stay behind for coffee and found the people they met friendly and welcoming. There was one person at the church who did recognise them although fortunately, this recognition was not reciprocated. This person was Detective Inspector Christine Powers, now living under her married name. Very sensibly, Christine did not identify herself to Hardman and Frank but observed with interest over the next few weeks how well they settled into church life. Indeed, they settled in surprisingly well. Being of retirement age, they were able to join the midweek lunch club where they started to build up a social circle of friends whom they really liked and admired. It was painful for them to be unable to say much about their own past lives. They even volunteered their services to collect and deliver food for the mini food hub which was St Giles' version of a foodbank.

Hardman and Frank used to discuss the things the Vicar had said in his Sunday morning sermons.

"I'm curious to know why the Vicar is so insistent that everyone at church is sinful and in great need of confessing their sins," puzzled Hardman. "Yes, it certainly applies to us but all the other people I've met at church seem to be paragons of virtue who don't commit sin."

"Well, he's made a pretty conclusive case for Jesus being truly human but also being God, living in the body of a man, and has shown us that the evidence that he rose from the dead on Easter Day is absolutely conclusive. It would appear that the main reason God came to earth in the person of Jesus was actually to die as if he were being punished on our behalf. In a strange way, the punishment he bore is the one we should be bearing for any sins we've committed."

This continued to puzzle Hardman (who was now known in church circles as Richard) until the pair attended a rather special mission service, held after they had been going St Giles for some months. Members of the congregation came to the front to give what Richard and Frank discovered were called testimonies, that is, significant religious experiences they had had in their own lives. Richard and Frank found one of these testimonies absolutely electrifying. It was given by one, Jason Brockhurst, whom Richard and Frank knew by sight but hadn't thus far made close personal contact.

Jason informed the congregation that he had been the company secretary of a local engineering firm which manufactured farm machinery among other items important to rural life. In this position, Jason had found it fairly easy to steal from his firm until his brother-in-law, who also worked at the firm, discovered what he was doing. During the row with his brother-in-law which followed this discovery, Jason picked up a paper punch from the desk and struck his brother-in-law. As he fell, the brother-in-law's head struck the sharp corner of the desk and he was dead when he hit the floor.

Jason described how he had been tried for manslaughter and having pleaded guilty and expressed contrition for what he had done, he was given the relatively light sentence of three years in jail but was released after serving two years in the light of his good conduct.

Jason explained how valuable his time in prison had been. He had spent quite a bit of time with the prison chaplain, bemoaning the fact that what he had done was irredeemable and he would be consigned to hell. The chaplain explained to Jason that this was not necessarily the case. Quoting King David as someone he considered as one of the worst characters in the Bible, committing adultery and compounding this with an act of murder to conceal his crime, the chaplain explained that because of his genuine contrition, he was forgiven by God. David expressed his relief in receiving this forgiveness for his acknowledged guilt in some of the psalms he wrote. The chaplain assured Jason that there is no crime which is beyond forgiveness. God came to earth in the form of the man, Jesus, to take the punishment for Jason's sin upon himself.

Jason went on to say that while in prison, he made a commitment to entrust Jesus with the rest of his life and as a result, he experienced a wonderful sense of freedom as if he were starting a totally new life. Since that time, his life had been filled with an unexplainable sense of peace and joy as he lived, not to satisfy his own needs and desires, but to fulfil whatever purpose he could for Jesus who now controlled his life.

As Richard and Frank listened to this, they craved this sense of freedom and forgiveness in their own lives for, like Jason, they considered that the sins they had committed were irredeemable. No, they had never actually caused anyone's death and the targets for their thefts were invariably rich bodies who could bear the loss. None the less, everything they had done had been in their own selfish interests. A verse came to their minds from a hymn which was often sung at the church,

> *To God be the glory, great things He hath done,*
> *So loved He the world that he gave us His Son.*

> *The vilest offender who truly believes,*
> *that moment from Jesus a pardon receives.*

Richard and Frank made an appointment to see the Vicar to talk about their personal spiritual predicament. The Vicar, who had come to like Richard and Frank without knowing about their previous lives of crime, could see how genuine they were in wishing to rectify their past mis-spent lives. He showed no sign of shock when they described their criminal activities but rather surprise at the audacious heists they'd carried out between them.

"There are just four simple steps which need to be taken so that you can enjoy the same experience as Jason," the Vicar explained. "You have already taken the first step which everyone must take but many find difficult. You have **ACKNOWLEDGED** that you are sinners with no possibility of making restitution for your sins yourselves. You need to **BELIEVE** that God in the form of Jesus came to earth with the express purpose of redeeming you from the consequence of these sins. It shouldn't be so difficult to recognise that Jesus was indeed God, living as a human because he performed a miracle which only God could do. He prophesised that he would be executed as if he was a sinner but would rise from the dead three days later. Careful examination by the world's most distinguished scholars have assured us that the resurrection really did take place as Jesus had prophesied. It's now accepted as the most authenticated fact of history.

Thirdly, you have to **COMMIT** yourselves to this belief, both in your minds, the way you think, and in your words, the way you speak of Jesus to others. Finally, you must **DEDICATE** your lives to Jesus. How do you do this? Well, Jason has explained in his testimony that he wears a bracelet on which are inscribed the letters, '**WWJD**' which stand for 'What Would Jesus Do?'. As you live your lives, you continually have to make decisions about your actions. If we study the life of Jesus, set out in the Bible, we can know him, almost like a brother, and this will enable us to make life's big moral decisions.

I've said a lot but what I've said is important and worth remembering. The four key words which may be called the ABCD of salvation are :-

ACKNOWLEDGE, BELIEVE, COMMIT, DEDICATE."

Richard and Frank had been listening intently to all this. They really wanted to experience the joy that shone out of Jason when he gave his testimony and now realised that their previous lifestyle didn't disqualify them from experiencing this joy themselves.

After the Vicar had said a prayer over them, they left the Vicar to think about what he had said. It was simple and straightforward and it all rang true. It didn't take long for them to come to a conclusion. Two days later, they returned to the Vicarage to tell him that they had decided to dedicate the rest of their lives to Jesus. The Vicar was delighted and asked them if they were prepared to share this with the congregation the following Sunday. They were prepared to do this but at the moment, they felt they couldn't share the details of their life of crime. Sufficient for them to say that they had been notorious criminals. Things were soon to happen which enabled Richard and Frank to feel able to say more to their new friends at St Giles about their notorious past.

Later that year, Richard and Frank arrived earlier than usual at Oakenhampton to attend the Sunday service, very much earlier before most folks were up. Was this because they had failed to put their clocks back the previous evening at the time of year when Autumn sets in? It was a lovely morning and they decided to use the time before the church service started to explore the town with which they had only superficial familiarity. As they turned up a side street, they were alarmed to see through a downstairs window, the flames of a fire which seemed out of control.

"Quick!" commanded Richard, "Phone 999! I'll try to get into the house."

Richard was not a stranger to housebreaking. He broke the front door window with a large stone lying near by and reached inside to release the Yale lock. He entered the house. The hallway was rapidly filling with smoke. Frank had alerted the fire service and was close behind. Frank tried to open the living room door but the handle was too hot to touch.

'The door's best left closed,' he thought. 'It'll act as a temporary fire break.'

Richard had made his way upstairs through the thickening smoke. Frank opened the door at the end of the hallway. This door handle was not hot. A frightened dog ran out into the front garden. He opened the back door. The key had been left in the lock.

'Hopefully, air coming into the house will clear some of the smoke,' he thought.

Frank opened the door to the other downstairs room. No-one was there.

He made his way upstairs. He could make out Richard, coming out of an upstairs bedroom carrying a child. He went into another room where he could see through the now thickening smoke, a woman asleep on the bed. He shook her awake.

"Fire!" he shouted. "Get out of the house!"

He went into the third room where another child was asleep on the bed. He awakened the child, picked him up and made his way back on to the landing. The panic stricken woman had also made her way on to the landing.

"My friend has already taken one child out," he cried out through the smoke to the woman. "Are there any more children up here?"

"No!" she responded.

"Then make your way out as quickly as possible," he commanded.

She started downstairs through the smoke which was now quite thick and Frank followed her out of the front door. By now, a fire engine had arrived and the firefighters were busy unravelling their hoses. A small crowd started to gather. The two children, now fully awake, huddled against their mother who was both shocked at what was happening but relieved to have her children safe and close to her. Richard and Frank had inhaled quite a bit of smoke and were coughing heavily. Two ambulances pulled up. The mother and her children left in one and Richard and Frank, the other. They were taken to North Cotswolds Hospital on the Stow Road, Moreton-in-the-Marsh.

Firefighters deal with fire
at Mrs Boyd's house

The family who had been rescued were Mrs Boyd and her children, Jennifer and Stuart. In normal circumstances, Richard and Frank would have recognised them by sight as fellow members of St Giles Church. They would have also seen Mrs Boyd at the mini food hub, run by the church, where Richard and Frank helped with the distribution of food to needy families. Mrs Boyd had been introduced to the church and the mini food hub by Christine Powers who had played an important part in exposing a scam which was causing Mrs Boyd a serious loss of money. This had been part of a murder investigation some time earlier in which Christine had been lead detective.

Mrs Boyd and the children were discharged from hospital the following day. They had been rescued before the smoke had seriously infiltrated their bedrooms and were declared fully fit. Richard and Frank, who had spent much longer in the thickest of the smoke than the young family, were kept in hospital for a further twenty-four hours but by then, they too were deemed fully fit to be discharged. Frank had had to have the hand he burned on a downstairs door handle dressed but no serious injury had been incurred. Mrs Boyd and the children had to be put up by friends until the smoke damage could be cleared and any necessary repairs carried out to the house. The cause of the fire appeared to be the malfunction of a plug-in air freshener. Although neat, compact and effective at freshening the air, these have been the cause of several fires and are therefore, not generally recommended for use.

After their rescue of the Boyd family, Richard and Frank became regarded as great heroes at St Giles. People had already warmed to them after hearing the testimonies of how they had become Christians but now, Richard and Frank felt able to give much fuller testimonies. Instead of just describing themselves as former criminals, they fascinated the congregation by describing some of their audacious heists in great detail but stressing how sincerely they regretted the selfishness of their actions and ambitions while living in a world full of needy people. Young people in the congregation were particularly intrigued by Richard and Frank's exploits. They described how the way the authorities of Salisbury and Lincoln cathedrals had given them the responsibility of making restitution for the money they had extorted, had completely refocused their attitude to life. They had become aware of the better use to which the money could be put in helping the world's most destitute people. Much as they would have liked to describe the way they stole the Crown of England, they desisted from doing this. The only reason they hadn't been prosecuted was the fact that the story would have caused very serious embarrassment to those in the most senior positions in the establishment, including King Charles himself. Disclosure of this heist would have removed the reason which afforded them protection from prosecution.

Christine Powers now felt able to declare her identity to the pair and to disclose that she had paid a large part in thwarting the heists which had failed. Richard and Frank showed real delight at making her acquaintance in these circumstances. Richard had only vague memories of the police officer who had arrested him after the abduction of the Tower ravens.

"You can't know how grateful we are for the events that directed us away from our life of crime," declared Richard. "We can now live the so much more satisfying and wholesome life that we are learning from our Christian friends, here at St Giles." Frank warmly concurred with Richard's words.

The books published by Midhurst have been written by Dr Ray Filby who has had many years' experience of church life in a number of churches, fulfilling at various times the roles of Pathfinder Group Leader, Youth Fellowship Leader, Secretary to the Parochial Church Council, Churchwarden and Reader (Licensed Lay Minister). This experience is reflected in the stories he writes which embrace several genres, including historical fiction, short stories, Bible study, murder stories and romantic fiction. They are all available from Amazon in paperback or Kindle form.

The Sun and the Moon of Alexandria

This is a fictional biopic of Apollos, a missionary saint and one of St. Paul's co-workers. Although mentioned many times in the New Testament, little is known of the life and background of Apollos. Thus, there is scope to create a story which constructs a feasible account of Apollos' youth in Egypt, his journey to Israel, his conversion, his relationship with St. Paul, his missionary work and his marriage. The story culminates in his martyrdom. In situations where Apollos interacts with well-known Biblical characters, the narrative remains faithful to the New Testament account.

(This book is published by the Book Guild)

Parables, the Greatest Stories ever told - Retold

'The Greatest Stories ever told – Retold' focuses on the better known parables of Jesus and rewrites them as situations in modern life which correspond to the situations in Jesus' day, attempting to promote the same teaching that Jesus was giving in the original parable. Each parable is preceded by a modern translation of the original parable and followed by ten questions which are suitable for a person's private devotions or for use in the context of a group Bible study.

St. Columba's – Its Life and Its People

Churches are living organisms, each with their own distinctive patterns of life. While their members experience the same ups and downs in life as the population as a whole, their Christian faith results in their reacting to circumstances in a distinctive way.

This book is a set of short stories, some of which trace the unfolding of events which occur as part of church life, and others which recount the experience of individual church members. Readers are invited to consider the practical or ethical problems which arise in these stories and think how they themselves might have dealt with or reacted to these situations.

The Countess who should have been Queen

Margaret Plantagenet was born near the end of the Wars of the Roses. As the daughter of the brother of King Edward IV, a situation could well have arisen when she or her brother, Edward, had a claim to the throne. Margaret was not ambitious to become Queen but was happy to marry a commoner and settled as an enlightened landowner with her husband in Berkshire. Margaret became Queen Catherine of Aragon's chief lady-in-waiting and was awarded a peerage to become Countess of Salisbury. Margaret faithfully supported Catherine right through her reign and as far as she could when Catherine was sent to live in isolation after her divorce. One of Margaret's sons, Reginald, became a prominent churchman and angered the King by writing a treatise, heavily critical of Henry VIII, the way he had divorced Catherine and taken over the Church of England. Reginald was living out of reach of Henry on the continent so Henry vented his wrath on Margaret and her family.

Consequences of Immature Love

Boy-Girl, Man-Woman relationships cement our society. Because these relationships are seldom straightforward, they provide scope for an indefinite number of works of fiction. In this novel, you are invited to follow the amorous adventures of Georgina Matthews and Arthur Gray from the time they leave school and start at university until they ultimately marry the partner for whom they seemed destined from the outset.

The story told might be of special interest to a young person embarking on the minefield of love and courtship as they consider the factors which led to the success or failure of the relationships encountered in this novel. Ethical factors are involved and it is significant that a shared Christian faith led to the final happy outcome.

Soldiers, Saints and Sinners

'*Soldiers, Saints and Sinners*' is a collection of fictitious stories, featuring some of the minor characters whom Jesus encountered in his ministry. It attempts to suggest how their backgrounds might have been important in the way they led to their encounter with Jesus and the way these encounters furthered the progress of Jesus' ministry. Each story is preceded by a modern Biblical translation of the passage which recounts their appearance on the scene where Jesus was ministering and is followed by five questions which are suitable for a person's private devotions or for use in the context of a group Bible study.

The Tasks of Chronavon

When sensible twelve-year-olds, Alfred and Alice meet a mysterious angel called Chronavon in the vestry of their church, it seems someone is playing a practical joke on them. After all, angels don't just pop up in church vestries to enlist the help of two young people to journey back in time to prevent a devilish time traveller from altering the course of history. Yet it soon becomes clear that Chronavon's incredible story is true. As Alfred and Alice are whisked backwards through the centuries, they become immersed in the rich customs and costumes of the past through Henry III's troubled reign, the insecurity of Princess Elizabeth before she became Queen Elizabeth I and the Civil War between the Cavaliers and Roundheads. 'The Tasks of Chronavon' is an exciting, informative tale for young readers which effortlessly weaves fact and fiction with a sprinkling of humour and shows how little human values have changed over time.

The Evil Occupants of Easingdale Castle

Teenager, Jason, and his friends, Bill, Becky and Liz, are recruited by an unusual messenger to pit their wits against an international gang of forgers, occupying their local castle. The gang are intent on destabilising the British economy by flooding the country with forged £20 notes which could pass off as the real thing. The gang is well equipped with hi-tech machines.

It remains to be seen whether Jason and his friends, who are also technically knowledgeable, can outwit the gang.

Technology will have advanced since this book was written and young readers are invited to consider whether they could have done better than Jason and his friends with equipment now available.

The Evil Emir of Transoxiana

Becky meets with her special friends, Jason, Bill and Liz, to tell them she is being posted to Transoxiana. She needs to explain exactly where she will be working, that she will be accompanied by Jason and that she will be spending some time with her Kyrgyz penfriend, Askari, and her husband, Temier.

During Becky's stay with Askari, Temier falls foul of an extremist Islamic cleric, the self-styled, Emir of Transoxiana. The resourcefulness of Becky and Jason, helped by Bill and Liz who travel out to join them, is needed to keep Askari and Temier safe from the Evil Emir. In spite of the danger being faced, they all manage to have the experiences in Transoxiana which make their stay both exciting and enjoyable.

A Church like Cluedo

After graduating from college as a civil engineer, Annette Owen had hoped to work in the developing world under the auspices of a missionary society. When this door to Christian service was closed, she applied to become an ordained minister but was turned down by the selection committee. She was however able to exercise a very fulfilled ministry as a clergy wife. Unfortunately, her clergy husband had dark secrets in his life of which Annette was totally unaware until a situation arose which resulted in murder being committed. The impact of this had an unexpected effect on the course of Annette's life.

Inspector Sinclair and Sergeant Powers' most interesting cases

This account of some interesting cases solved by the detective duo, Inspector Sinclair and Sergeant Powers, is not a normal 'whodunnit' in which the murderer is not revealed until the very end when the detective reveals the clues which he or she alone has picked up to solve the case without sharing their significance with the reader until the very end.

The stories in this book are divided into sections, a list of those involved to help the reader keep track of the characters,

'the Event' which describes the situation when the murder took place,

'the Investigation' which describes the systematic way in which the detectives investigated the case and

'the Evidence' in which the crucial evidence by which a cast iron case against the murderer was built up, is reviewed.

An Insight into the Gospels and the Book of Acts

'An Insight into the Gospels and the Book of Acts' is an overview of the themes, contents, emphases, and structure of the first five books of the New Testament. While there is so much similarity in the stories and teaching in each of the gospels, this book contrasts the way each gospel is written and presented. It highlights the quite remarkable differences which exist between each of the gospels as they are directed to different audiences and have different primary objectives. The book is presented with the main content of the book appearing on the right hand (odd numbered) pages and supportive texts placed opposite the relevant passages on the left hand pages.

The Warrior and the Bride

This work of Biblical fiction is largely set in the period covered by the 2nd Book of Samuel and the 1st Book of Kings. It features Benaiah and Abishag, two characters who had important roles to play in serving King David and his successor. Although a work of fiction, the author has tried to make it consistent with the Biblical narrative and references are provided wherever the story is related to a Biblical event. The author realises that minor inconsistencies occur in the text but then, minor inconsistencies can be found in the Bible itself. There is no indication in the Bible that the two main characters were in any way related but nothing in the Bible specifically states that they were not.

Consequences of Careless Cyber Crime

Detective Inspector Christine Powers and her partner, Detective Sergeant Bill Matthews, are involved in a missing person enquiry, but this turns into a murder investigation when the missing person is found buried in a shallow grave by a layby. They have their suspicions but no leads on the way the murder was carried out or the motive. However, an unexpected lead does come to light when they start to investigate a cyber crime which proves to be linked with the murder.

Puzzles, Quiz and Activities Suitable for Social Events

Volumes 1, 2, 3, 4, 5 & 6

These books consist of a set of puzzles, quiz and activities which the author designed for use at a monthly social event organised by St. Michael's, Church, Budbrooke, in the Community Centre in the part of the parish known as Chase Meadow. People who have opted to take part really seem to have enjoyed these activities which are interesting rather than extremely challenging. While a good general knowledge is helpful in completing some of the activities, they are not designed to expose people's ignorance as data sheets and appropriate reference books like atlases are made available to help participants find any information needed. Thus, the activities are educational.

The socials run at Chase Meadow are not restricted to church members but all and sundry are invited as part of the church outreach. With many of the activities, a final stage often involves deciphering a phrase, quote or saying. As the socials are sponsored by the church, many of the quotes to be deciphered are Biblical texts. However, anyone choosing to use these ideas could quite easily modify the final stage and use a secular quote rather than a Biblical text to be deciphered.